Natural State Escape

By Tamra Kidd

Text Copyright © 2014 Tamra Kidd

All Rights Reserved

Note From The Author

I originally wrote this book on a whim for my friend and relative, Gentry Hipp, as a fun promotion for his business, Hipp Modern Builders, that actually does exist in Mountain View Arkansas. The more I wrote, the more it developed, and what was originally going to take two or three months, ended up taking about eight months to write and then longer after editing.

In this book, as well as future books, I have left out foul language so that anyone can enjoy a good story for what it's worth without having to cringe at one of life's too common and overused forms of self-expression, which to me can ruin a book or a movie and decrease the size of your audience. I would like to explain though, that although this is a work of fiction, some of the events in the book are gory and disturbing in nature. In small rural communities we forget or don't realize that events, like the ones described in this book, do happen. Serial killers do exist. If anything, I hope that by reading this it would make you aware of your surroundings and of people. Also, to give credit to the dedicated work of law enforcement, criminal profilers, and the study of behavioral science, which tries to help us understand the mind of the criminal, how they think and why they do what they do.

Gentry and I have always liked horror movies and I thought this would be a fun way to capture everyone's imagination as well as to promote his business, and to describe some beautiful places in Arkansas where Gentry and I both grew up. I hope you enjoy the story.

Disclaimer

This is a work of fiction. The only name that is an actual person is Gentry Hipp, for whom the book was written. Other names, characters, places within the cities mentioned in the story, and incidents either are the product of the author's imagination or are used fictitiously, and any resemblance to actual persons, living or dead, businesses other than Hipp Modern Builders, companies, events, or locales is entirely coincidental.

While the author has made every effort to provide accurate phone numbers and website addresses when this work was published, neither the publisher nor author assumes and responsibility for errors, or changes that may have occurred after publication. The publisher does not have any control over and does not assume any responsibility for author or third party websites or their content.

Planning The Vacation

Chapter 1

"So where do you wanna go on vacation this year?" Frank asked Shelly, his physically fit, green eyed, brunette wife of three years, as they ate a breakfast of cereal and orange juice in their apartment overlooking Central Park.

"I don't know. Where do you want to go?" Shelly asked him shoveling a big spoonful of cereal into her mouth smiling.

Looking down at the sea of cars under the smog choked sky, and around at the steel and concrete buildings, Frank thought to himself, as he ran his fingers through his dirty blonde hair, that was just long enough and "wispy" as Shelly called it, to touch his collar and fall over his ears, but in a professional way, about how nice it would be to get out into the country where there was no noise, no pollution, and no millions of people all crammed together in the congested city. Finally he came out of his daydream and looked over at her and said; "Let's go to the country. And I don't just mean upstate either, I mean WAY out to the country. Let's go to....Arkansas!"

"Arkansas?" She asked with a smile, still eating, "Why Arkansas?"

"Well, I figure you can't get much more country than that! And it's someplace we've never been before. It's known for outdoor experiences such as hunting, fishing, and beautiful scenery. That's why they call it the 'Natural State'

. Hauling up another spoonful, she asked, "Have you

read up on it on the net?"

"I have not; he stated, pointing his index finger in the air, but I will today and we can talk about it tonight when we get home from work." He said; swallowing down the last of his orange juice. He got up from the table and holding back his blue tie with the black, diagonal pinstripes, with one hand, leaned over to give her a quick kiss across the table. "Hope I have a little time in between cases and court to do a little research."

"O.K. that sounds like a plan", she said as she kissed him back. "I'll look at it too and we'll see how many things we can find to see and do and make a decision about where in Arkansas we'd like to go."

She quickly rose from the table, since they had almost made themselves late talking, and put her tennis shoes on to go to her job as an exercise instructor. It would be a long day for both of them and would be late in the evening when they both made it home.

They left their apartment catching cabs in opposite directions. Frank had worked at a prestigious law firm for the last seven years, right in the middle of Manhattan, as a criminal law attorney. He started working there as soon as he graduated law school and had just been offered the position to become a partner in the firm. They handled the worst cases, from gang violence, to homicides of all varieties, and there was no end to them in the city. He had worked very hard and had won over eighty five percent of his cases and was ready for a rest.

He had put in for vacation earlier on in the year, while

it was still cold. It was now the first week of April and his two week vacation started on the second week of May, so they didn't have long to make up their minds where they wanted to go. Shelly could take off work about any time she wanted to, since she was the owner of her own business, as she had a degree in Health Fitness that helped people adopt and maintain healthy lifestyles. She had clients who paid her by the hour just to help them learn how to exercise, and to teach them how to eat healthy meals. It had proven to be a lucrative job and she really loved it.

Frank and Shelly met at a neighborhood restaurant at dinner one evening. She was just finishing up with a client, informing her on how to choose the right foods in a restaurant, when Frank, who was sitting in the booth behind them, overheard their conversation and was interested. When he heard Shelly say goodbye to her client, Frank walked over and started asking her questions about what he was eating.

His diet was horrible and Shelly cringed at what was in his plate. He had ordered the most fattening thing on the menu, chicken fried steak with extra gravy, and French fries also smothered in gravy. He had used the salt shaker liberally, and to top it off, had a large piece of pecan pie with whipped cream on the top, and a large Coke. She told him she hoped he would make it out of the restaurant without having a heart attack, stroke, or both, and said if he was interested in becoming one of her clients to give her a call and she handed him her card.

Frank took the card and, laughing out loud, told her that he really wasn't interested in becoming a client, but wondered if she was free and would like to go out sometime to a movie and a much more healthy meal. Shelly was surprised at the offer, and found his smile and eyes to be very genuine. She told him she was indeed free and would love to. She promised to give him some free advice on eating healthy when they went out. That was three years ago and many healthy meals later. Since that day, they had gotten married and had moved into his apartment while they saved enough money to buy a house. They had more than enough money now, and had been looking for the "perfect" home in the last few months.

When they finally returned home that night, the day had been a busy one for both, but somehow, they had each gotten a chance to look up Arkansas and several of the state's interesting and beautiful places. For such as small and state, Arkansas seemed to have a lot to offer in the way of what they were looking for in their vacation.

"Alright, what have you got?" Shelly asked Frank, rubbing her hands together, as they both settled down on their oversized couch with their laptop.

"Well, I found Little Rock, of course. Being the capital, it has lots of stuff to see and do. Then, I found a place west of there, Hot Springs, which sounds nice. It has bath houses and quaint old hotels, a horse racing track with casino style gaming, and a wax museum. They have a flower garden to tour and a lake...Hamilton, I believe. How about you? Did you find anything?" He asked her with his reading glasses down at the tip of his nose and his brows raised, eyes looking up over the glasses.

"I found a town that is a resort area called Heber Springs; Shelly countered, where there is also a lake, the Greers Ferry Lake, and also another smaller resort, Greers Ferry, that the lake is named for. It's known for boating and fishing and is quite the spot for summer campers and hunting in the winter."

They looked over each other's information and talked about the different towns and what activities there were to do and how the town looked. Frank had a look on his face of deep concentration and finally told her that there was one more place he found, but hadn't really had time to research it. It was a town called Mountain View.

"Mountain View, "Shelly said wistfully. "Sounds pretty."

They clicked on to the website and looked at all the things to do. There was an Ozark Folk Center where they had live music and folk singing. There was a Court Square that also had live singing and historic buildings with several restaurants in the area and shops that you could walk to with antiques, and wood crafts. There was even a place called Blanchard Springs Caverns just a few miles away, which was basically an underground cave with beautiful rock formations that had been growing for hundreds of years. There was trout fishing from the river, canoeing, and hiking on the Sylamore Creek, and all types of bed and breakfasts, motels, and cabin rentals all over the little town.

"It kinda does doesn't it? Frank smiled; removing his glasses and putting the earpiece between his lips, pausing to think. We both enjoy hiking and canoeing, and the caverns sound neat, huh?" He asked looking over at her.

"Yes, and the Court Square and the old buildings sound quaint and romantic. Like going back in time almost." She answered as she leaned over closer to Frank, putting her head on his shoulder.

"I know, the other places sound interesting too, Frank agreed as he put his arm around her, pulling her closer; and they're not that far away from Mountain View. Maybe we could drive to a couple of them just to see how they look, but you know, I'm tired of resorts and lots of people. I would really like to just enjoy peace and quiet. Be able to spend some time alone with you and enjoy the beauty of the outdoors and not hear all the city noise. Take our time and not be rushed doing things."

"Me too. It sounds like a wonderful place. Let's go there!" Shelly exclaimed.

"I'll make the flight reservations the first thing tomorrow!" Frank said as he grabbed her and kissed her. This would be their first real vacation together as a married couple, besides their honeymoon. He was excited to get to spend time with her in a sleepy little town and forget about work and people for a while, and forget about the dangers of the city. There was lots to do before they left and they still had to decide on a place to stay once they got there.

It had been a busy day for Frank. He had been in court a lot longer than he had expected. The defendant's client, a known "Crip" was on trial for the murder of a rival gang member of the "Bloods", and even though all the evidence was stacked against him, they had a hung jury. The verdict finally came in when one of the undecided jurors finally, to the delight of all the other jurors and Frank as well, decided that he was indeed guilty, and the bailiff gave the judge their decision. Murder in the first degree with a deadly weapon, which got him a sentence of life without parole in the federal prison system.

After six hours in court, Frank finally got to go back to the office and file some paperwork, and get ready for the next day's case. As he was walking down the hallway of the building his law office was in, a colleague stopped him in the hallway and congratulated him on winning the case.

"You did a good job in there Frank. I heard about the jury. Where do they get these people? That one juror must have been the most uneducated kook I've ever heard of!" He remarked.

"You're telling me! Thanks Harry. Frank said smiling, then added; I'm so glad that I'll be going on vacation in a few weeks. I really need a break."

"Where are you going? Some place tropical and romantic?" He asked.

"Mountain View, Arkansas!"

"Whoa! You really are getting away aren't ya?"

"Yes. Frank knew it would probably sound crazy, so he explained. I'm ready for some peace and quiet. Maybe do a little fishing and hiking. They have a lot of nice sounding things to do there. We just want to relax."

"Nothing wrong with that. Hey, did you say Mountain View?" Harry asked.

"I did."

"Hmmm.... Small world, but I think my wife has some family there and they have some cabins or lodges out in that area. I might be able to get you one for free if you're interested?"

"That sounds great....sure!"

"Hang on a second and I'll call her." Frank sat down in one of the black leather chairs at the end of the hallway in the lobby that was designed for present and potential clients to sit and wait on someone to see them. He was glad he had run into Harry and hoped that he could get them a cabin. Not that they were broke, but they could save a lot of money and do so much more. Shelly would be impressed. He waited as Harry dialed her number.

Harry called his wife and asked her if she really did have family that lived in Mountain View, Arkansas or was he dreaming. Then after hearing her answer, which confirmed true enough she did, he asked if she thought her uncle would mind if Frank and his wife stayed in the cabin. He reminded her that her uncle had given them an open ended invitation to come and stay. Harry's wife said she would give him a call right after she and Harry hung up.

Harry closed his outdated cell phone that Frank had made fun of him having, more than once, and not upgrading to a more modern type of cell phone like a smart phone. He was telling Frank all about her family. They were "hill people" as Harry put it, and lived in the mountains or Ozarks, as it was known in Arkansas. They were self-made industrialists, that is, they had their own business created by buying several acres of land and then building cabins on it to rent out.

It wasn't more than five or ten minutes that she called back and gave Harry her uncle's phone number to give to Frank. She said her uncle would be happy for them to come and stay in one rent free. He said that any friend of Harry's was a friend of his, and since she and Harry never had time to come, that whoever he sent was welcome. Frank took the number and thanked Harry graciously and went to finish up his day.

On his way home, Frank took out the card with Harry's wife's uncle's cell phone number, and gave him a call, to confirm for himself, that it was alright that they stay. Harry had told Frank that his wife's uncle's name was Cecil and that he was one of the nicest guys you would ever meet. Frank dialed the number with the 870 area code, and the phone began to ring. It only took a couple of rings before a country sounding voice answered the phone.

"Hello from the "Hills and Hollers" of Mountain View Arkansas. This is Cecil, can I help you?"

"Yes, Cecil….my name is Frank and a colleague of mine spoke to his wife earlier whom I believe is your niece?" Frank started with a smile. They're telling me that it's okay for my wife and I to stay in one of your cabins there in Mountain View on our vacation in May."

"Well, hello Frank! Cecil said in a happy voice. Yes, that niece of mine and her husband are always busy and are never able to get down here, but we welcome them and their friends. When are you lookin' to come out?"

"Somewhere on either May 8th or 9th. That would give us a day to get packed and rested, and make any mistakes on the way!" Frank laughed.

"Well, it's always wise to give yourself extra time. I think you're gonna like what I'm about to tell you.

That's a great time for you to come out. Cecil explained. Me and my family will be going out of state a day or two after you get here, on the 10th of May, to be exact, for about three weeks, and won't even be on the place at all. We're going on our own vacation to the beach in Alabama. Cecil laughed. We kinda get tired of the "mountain life". So, you'll have the whole place to yourself, because we've blocked all of our reservations to the general public, but since family has sent you, then you'll be treated just like you were our kinfolk. We'll meet you when you get here, let you pick out a cabin of your choice, and then give you the key to it."

"Oh, wow! That's really great! Are you sure it's not a problem…I mean. We're honest people and will take care of your cabin like it was our own." Frank stammered, not believing their good luck.

"Well, thank you, son I believe you would, and we might just work out a couple of things when you get here. Nothing that will take away time from your vacation, and it would be much appreciated. Just give us a call when you get to Mountain View and I'll tell you how to get here.

We'll be looking forward to meeting you and your wife." Cecil said with sincerity.

They finished their conversation and Frank finally got home

a little after 6PM to find that Shelly was already there and was sitting on the couch with her laptop. She was book marking all of the things she wanted to see and do in Mountain View. Frank sat down beside her and excitedly told her that she would never believe the conversation he had just had on the phone. She was thrilled and couldn't wait to tell all of her friends and family, that they would be staying in a cabin with the business name of "Hills and Hollers", and that it would be free. She couldn't wait to start packing and had already made a large list of things she thought they would need for the trip. Frank thought it was a good thing that the cabin was free, because it would cost that much in rent just to buy what Shelly had put on her list. They needed to make a trip shopping this weekend and buy a few things they couldn't live without.

After relaxing for a while and watching TV, they wrote down a list of the things they thought they really needed, the first thing being a good First Aid kit. Shorts, tank tops, plus jeans and hiking boots. A couple of nice outfits to go eat out in, as well as their laptops and cell phones, digital cameras and all of the chargers. Shelly said she would never fit everything in the two small suitcases she'd had since before they got married, so she needed a new duffel bag, and so did Frank. Then they wrote down all of the things they each wanted to do. They wanted to first take a look at the cabins and pick one out. Then they wanted to drive around in the town and just see what it looked like and get a feel where everything was. They wanted to go to Blanchard Springs Caverns and the Ozark Folk Center. They wanted to go hiking and canoeing on the White River and Swimming at Sylamore Creek.

They wanted to see the Court Square and listening to music was a must, as well as shopping along the street in old down town Mountain View. One day they wanted to drive out to Heber Springs and also rent a boat on Greers Ferry Lake. Beyond that they didn't make any plans so they could leave it open to see what else they might find to do. The whole thing was an adventure. Tomorrow was Saturday and they had made plans to go shopping the whole weekend. They were both excited. There was a Bass Pro Shop in Massachusetts that wouldn't take too long to get to, and their local Wal-Mart. Frank figured they could find everything they needed at those two stores. They had both taken a lot of joking from friends and coworkers about their vacation destination, and had both been told, in no uncertain terms, that it would be the most boring vacation either of them had ever had, and that they would be glad to get back home to the city. They took it all good naturedly and kept making plans. They had both lived in the city all of their lives and the closest thing they had ever gotten to living the country life was in upstate New York. They were ready to experience some real country living that hadn't been created to look pretty by human planning, but by divine design. After doing their research all evening and planning, not to mention their whole day at work, Frank and Shelly finally collapsed into bed that night. They were so glad it was the weekend. They would both be able to sleep in later than usual, but they still wanted to get up early because they had a lot of shopping to do. Shelly sat her alarm clock by the bed for 7AM. She hadn't thought about it until just that moment, right before rolling over to go to sleep, and she asked; "Did you get us plane tickets, Frank?"

"I'm sorry, I forgot to tell you; He said raising up in bed, Mountain View doesn't have a full sized airport, so we'll have to take a small jet instead. It cost a little extra but with the expense we're saving on a free cabin, it's no big deal, so yes, I got us a flight on a sweet little jet!"

"Great! That will be much more fun than a big commercial plane with lots of people on it anyway, and much faster. That's awesome! This is going to be so much fun!" With that, she rolled over with his arm draped across her, and they both seemed to fall instantly to sleep. Frank dreamed of a little cabin with a stream running nearby, and of big trees that surrounded them on all sides. It was quiet and peaceful with nothing but clear blue sky to look up at, with just the sound of the birds chirping in the trees and the smells of the outdoors. Somewhere in his dream, he thought he heard Shelly calling to him, but he couldn't make out what she was saying, and there was a dark cloud over the cabin, then everything went black. Frank woke up with a start and looked at the clock on his nightstand. It was only 4AM. He still had three more hours to sleep before they had to get up and go shopping for their vacation. He recalled that he had been dreaming about a cabin, and that everything had gotten dark. He made a mental note to buy some flashlights, in case a storm came and the electricity went out, and maybe some matches in case there was a fireplace, and they had to make a fire for warmth or wanted to make a fire to be cozy. Before he knew it, he had dozed off again, and the next time he awoke, it was really time to get up.

Killing In The Delta

Chapter 2

In a rural delta town that was forty minutes from the Arkansas border, an arrest was being made in Tallulah Louisiana. Just hours before, in Eudora Arkansas, the southernmost tip of the state, a grisly scene was unfolding of a murder that had taken place, which had shocked the townspeople. It was actually the first murder of multiple murders that started in Eudora and ended on a fishing dock in Lake Providence, Louisiana.

The killer had been a local who lived in Tallulah, and was known to "have problems" with his temper. He had been involved in several assaults and domestic disturbances lately with people he didn't like, or had a history with, and anybody else who crossed him. Everyone was, to put it mildly, scared to death of him. He was a tall and well-built man, with broad shoulders, long arms, and big hands. He had a head of thick, dark brown hair and wasn't a bad looking guy, but always seemed to have a scowl on his face no matter when he was seen.

He was a hard worker at his job at the Wrench Right station as a "tire maintenance tech", and had been there for years. He had never given the boss or co-workers a day of trouble, but for no apparent reason, he had gone on an angry killing spree, that started sometime after he had left work that day. The last place anyone saw him, was at a restaurant in Eudora called the Southern Style Steakhouse and it was there that witnesses placed him at the scene of the crime.

There was a biker gang that had pulled up to the restaurant, and when everyone was questioned, no one at the restaurant saw or heard what happened as the killer was claiming his victim, but the biker gang stated that one of their members got up to go get something from his motorcycle during their meal, and never back in. Finally someone went to check and see what was taking him so long, and they found him sitting astraddle of his Harley, with his hands on the handle bars and his helmet in his lap. The only problem with that, was that his head was still in the helmet. It had been severed completely off of his neck, and left sitting right between his legs, at the base of the gas tank. The fellow biker that found him, turned and vomited into the bushes a few feet away and saw a man who was covered in blood getting into a truck, that later matched the description of a truck from another homicide report which had come in that night, and racing away.

On down the road about twenty miles away, there was a car that had pulled off the road, right next to a giant red sign in the shape of a piece of pizza, which read Pepperoni Pizza Palace. The driver apparently stopped to check to see if something was wrong with his car, because the trooper who found him, saw that the hood had been up, but when he stopped to check and see if anyone needed help, the body of a man was still halfway under the hood leaning over the motor, and a knife was sticking up out of his back, between his shoulder blades. The motor was still running and the side of his face, which had been lying on the engine block, had been cooked into a red mush, which was as messy as the pepperoni pizza slice that the car was parked under.

The knife was almost as big as a machete, and had bloody prints all over the handle. Though there wasn't much blood at the scene, except what was under the vehicle, which had dripped out of the victim after he had been stabbed. When they moved the body, the tip of the knife had gone all the way through, and it was sticking out through the front his shirt. Most of the bleeding had seemed to pool inside the victim's body, with the knife actually acting as a plug, keeping it from pouring out.

There were no witnesses at the scene, but the Louisiana state trooper and the East Carroll Parish Sheriff's Department would put out a reward for any credible information for any persons or vehicles that might have been seen stopped with that car.

At the Threads Cotton Plant, an old farmer was riding his tractor in from the field. It looked like he had made it to the tractor shed, and was about to walk out of the shed, when someone had ran into him with a bob truck and pinned him to the wall of the shed. His body was cut almost in half and he had a look of horror on his face. The worker who found him said, through tears and blubbering, that he would never forget, as he shook his head and wiped his eyes while telling the sheriff. The sheriff had already been out to view the body and didn't think he would ever forget it either. In all of his thirty two years of law enforcement, and six being the sheriff, he had never seen anything so grisly.

The police scanners had been going non-stop from Chicot County, in Eudora to East Carroll Parish, in Louisiana and beyond, ever since the first body had been found. To the people in "scanner world" it seemed like a bunch of separate incidences occurring all at once that night, and everyone wondered what had gotten into folks, but to the law enforcement world, they thought something entirely different. They just didn't want to say it yet, because they didn't want to scare the public. They wanted to be sure of what they had first.

They were hoping that the cotton farm murder was the last one, but when they got the call from the Sizzlin Shrimp, out by Lake Providence, they knew this wasn't separate calls, but was what they had first feared. This was the work of a serial killer.

There was already a crowd forming when the patrol car roared into the parking lot. The deputy got out and asked everyone to stay where they were, so as not to contaminate the crime scene, and went walking down to the fishing dock. There, at the very end of the dock was the body of a man that had been tied to the dock by his hands, and the rest of his body was hanging off into the water. At least what was left of it. He had several deep cuts in his abdominal area that had bled profusely, and had attracted the local lake alligators and turtles, and most of what was left of his body was mangled and torn to shreds. The deputy thought that the cotton farm murder was bad, but this topped that by a long shot.

He keyed up his mike and confirmed to dispatch to have the coroner and the sheriff dispatched to that location, and asked for extra back up for crowd control. He walked back up the dock and into the crowd of people who were standing next to the side of the restaurant. There was a mixture of fear and curiosity on their faces. He asked if any of them had any information they could give him and he took out his pocket notebook and started writing.

There wasn't anyone there who had been eating at the restaurant for more than the last fifteen to thirty minutes, so they had not seen anything out of the ordinary. The body had been found by a couple of boys who had been planning on going fishing, and had carried their poles and minnows out to the dock when they found the victim and turned and ran back to the Sizzlin Shrimp.

It didn't take long to establish a time line of the events that happened. It seemed the murders happened in order from Eudora, Arkansas, all the way down to the Lake Providence fishing dock. Also, more people had thought they saw an old gray Chevrolet pickup, either leaving the scene or headed down the road, around the same time each murder occurred, which would fit with the first witness's statement at the Southern Style Steakhouse in Eudora. So, a "BOLO" or "Be On The Lookout" had been issued for a vehicle fitting that description. It was the end of the month in April and the summer was just getting started and every sheriff's department had already gotten busier and would stay that way until winter.

This just added to the mix and they wanted to jump on this and catch this suspect, who they knew was a serial killer, as fast as they could before he killed someone else.

Before the next day, police got a tip that someone knew of a man fitting the description that the first witness had seen, and that he drove a truck similar to the one described.

He lived in Tallulah, behind and old warehouse in a run-down neighborhood, on the edge of town. Neighbors said he roared down Swamp Street, and came to a stop at his house, and had went straight to the water hose in his front yard. He had been covered in blood and hadn't even bothered to try and hide it. They saw him start hosing himself off in a fit, as if trying to scrub off his own skin, while talking to himself the whole time. It went on for a while, until he finally went in the house where he had remained since. The neighbors all thought it odd, but they didn't have scanners and weren't aware of what was going on, so nobody had reported it, keeping it to themselves until someone had turned on the news that evening, before going to bed, and saw the story. When questioned why no one turned it in, they replied for all they knew he could've just been wrestling with an alligator in the swamp and had got bitten, or that he had just killed a hog or some other animal. He was a loner and kept to himself and they respected his privacy and also admitted they were a little afraid of him.

    As soon as the Madison Parish Sheriff's Department got the news that the suspect lived in their city, there was a team of deputies dispatched to the house and the suspect, who was sleeping on the couch, was arrested for the murders.

    He was handcuffed, and placed in a patrol car that was pulled up in his front yard, and hauled off to jail.

    The suspect was fingerprinted, and the prints matched the prints found on the motorcycle helmet of the first victim. They also matched the prints found on the knife of the second victim, and on the steering wheel, and door of the truck that ran into the third victim. There were no fingerprints to be found on the fourth victim that was found on the fishing dock, but witnesses in the area claimed to have seen a truck parked near the Sizzlin Shrimp that matched the suspects truck, around the time that the murder occurred, and there was a partial footprint in the dirt, that matched the sole of one of the suspects shoes near the area where the truck was reported to have been parked.

Not only that, the suspect himself admitted to the crime and when asked why he killed them he made only one statement; "God told me to kill them". Law enforcement didn't quite know what to make of him, glancing back and forth at one another at his statement, shaking their heads as they walked away from his cell.

Later that week, he went before the judge and was sentenced to life in prison without the possibility of parole and would remain in the Madison Parish Sheriff's custody, until they got him housed into a prison in the next few days. He had no expression on his face as the judge handed down the decision.

Shackled and handcuffed, he was led into a jail cell of his own because he was such a violent offender. The cuffs and the shackles remained on, even though he was in a cell, and all sheets and blankets were removed from his cot to prevent him from the possibility of committing suicide. He sat down on his cot and waited for whatever came next. All there was to do was wait. Eventually, he would get a chance to escape and rid the world of more people that deserved to die, and the world was full of them. He marveled at how every single day people placed themselves in a position of harm's way and some of them escaped…but not all of them. The biker, for instance. He had been his first kill. He remembered that he had been in a daze all day at work that day. Nothing went wrong, it just felt that he was being pulled away. Like there was somewhere he was supposed to go, but he didn't know where. He felt an internal urge to fix people and the way they believed. People didn't want to believe in the right things anymore. They didn't want to believe in God. And God was real. His mother always believed in God and took him to church when he was a little boy. He had grown up and gotten busy working and had not gone with her to church as much over the years. He had also been dating. She had seemed like the perfect girlfriend. Well, that was a lie. She had been there for him when his mother had gotten diagnosed with cancer. She had been there for him after she had died, but as soon as he had started going to church again and had told her about the mission God had given him she grew angry. She argued with him that if God *was* real and as loving as the preacher said he was, then he wouldn't send Michael out to kill people for him. He tried to explain to her that God had disciples who would do his work for him just like Jesus had had disciples. She still disagreed with him and told him he was wrong and before he knew what she was doing, she had grabbed her things and left. That's when his world had changed. He had been thinking about it all day and knew what he had to do.

    He had no idea who it would be, but when he pulled into the Southern Style Steakhouse and saw the biker sitting on his motorcycle with the leather vest that said Devil Dogs, he could hear the voice that was becoming familiar say,

"That one." He parked his truck at the side of the restaurant and walked around to where the biker was. He was sitting astride the motorcycle and had gotten a map out of one of the side compartments when Michael had calmly walked up to him and asked him the question.

"Hi there. I was wondering if you could help me, man. I've just had the worst day of my life and I'm feeling a little suicidal. Can you help me?" He said with as much sincerity as he could summon.

The biker, caught off guard, looked up from his map and answered asking willingly what he could do to help him.

"Do you believe in God? I need you to pray with me?"

"Ummm, sorry buddy. I can't help you there, man."

With that Michael had nodded his head in mock acceptance and had turned to leave. He went back to his truck and reached behind the seat and got the knife. He went around the opposite side of the restaurant then up behind the second row of cars until he was right behind the biker.

He was still sitting there and had the map spread out across the gas tank looking down at it. He began to fold it back up. The paper gave a crinkling rattle as he tried to fold it back into place. Michael sprinted forwards and in one fluid motion, with one hand landing on the biker's forehead and the other slicing with the knife across his neck, the bikers head hung on by a thread. Michael severed that last hold, grunting with the effort. As a last sentiment, he placed the biker's hands on the handlebars and the biker's head on his own lap.

He had asked the same question of all of them that he

Had killed. The guy working on his car under the billboard sign that looked like pizza, had been even more deserving. Michael had put on his dark blue work coat after he had killed the biker, to hide the blood stains on his light blue shirt. His pants were a dark navy, so they weren't noticeable. He had parked his truck a few feet away from the stranded motorist and casually walked up and asked his question. When Michael had asked him if he believed in God, he had snorted and said that God was a joke. Michael had pretended not to care and had even started talking to the guy about what was wrong with his car and had pointed to a hose close to the radiator. Michael told him he could see a hole in it and when the guy went to reach for the hose, leaning as far down as he could get, Michael reached behind himself into the waistband of his jeans and grabbed the knife, slamming it down as hard as he could into the man's back. It was the same knife he had just used to cut off the biker's head and it still had some of the blood on it from the biker. After the kill, he was about to remove it but decided that he would use a different method the next time. He reasoned that maybe using the knife was too easy and that another way might give them a chance to change their mind because with the knife in his hands, their life was definitely over.

    At the cotton plant, Michael had followed the farmer from the field on his tractor. That was where he had talked to him was in the field. Michael had parked his truck at an abandoned building next to the road where the farmer had been attaching a plow to the tractor. Michael had walked up and asked him the question. The farmer had been nice about it, but had told Michael that he was Amish and followed the teachings of Joseph Smith, their prophet. They did not pray to the Christian God. He asked if he could help Michael in a different way, but Michael declined, thanked him, and walked back to his truck and just sat there. He waited until after the farmer had gotten almost back to the barn before he started up. Slowly he drove to the barn and parked behind it so that the farmer couldn't see him. He went inside the barn and over to a large truck in which they used to haul their grain. He tried the door and it opened. The keys were in the ignition. He climbed up inside and waited. The farmer had parked just inside the barn and got off of his tractor. He could see the farmer was detaching the plow and didn't know Michael was anywhere around. He had gotten the plow unhooked and was walking back in front of the tractor when Michael started the truck and roared towards him. The farmer was frozen in place. Michael braced for the impact and felt it when he hit. With the farmer pinned between the building and the truck, all signs of life leaving his body, Michael walked away. And lastly, his walk out on the fishing dock. He had actually pulled in there just to gather himself. This mission was hard work. He had gotten out of his truck and was walking past the Cyprus trees that lined the edge of the water which ran parallel to the highway when he passed the fishing dock. He could see a man sitting at the end of it with a fishing pole. As he got closer he could see the bottle of whiskey next to him. The man was quite noticeably drunk and laughed when Michael asked him the question and told him that he had come to the dock to do precisely that himself...drink himself to death. Michael asked him why wasn't he praying to God and the man answered that God himself wouldn't want to save him and even if he did, he wasn't about to beg for forgiveness of being a drunk because that was the only thing that had made him able to deal with life and kept him here this long. Michael, trying another approach, almost with curiosity asked, "But God loves you and forgives you of everything."

"I don't think he's gonna forgive me of this. The guy stammered as he took another long drink from the almost empty bottle of whiskey. There was a bag next to him with at least three more in it. He was crying.

"Do you believe in God? Michael asked once again.

"Yeah…crying and coughing so hard he could hardly speak. I don't want to go to hell, but I was so tired of living that I just couldn't stand it anymore. The bible says you'll go to hell if you commit suicide!"

Michael prodded once more, "If you believe in God, then go ahead and ask him for forgiveness and he will give it to you. No question. Just ask, and it shall be given."

"But I've already drank so much. I'm probably already dying." He wailed animatedly.

"But you're still here. Hurry. Say your prayers."

Amazingly the man got down on his knees right there on the dock and began to pray for forgiveness of everything he'd done his whole life. His voice getting louder by the second. He wailed and moaned for all of the transgressions he had caused and asked forgiveness that his life was such a mess. He prayed that God would forgive him because he didn't want to go to hell. That's when Michael grabbed him from behind and whispered in his ear that he was a disciple of

God and that he had been sent here to kill him. In Michael's understanding, the guy already believed in God and had asked forgiveness for his sins. That took care of one part. Michael would take care of the rest. He grabbed the neck of the whiskey bottle and swung it at one of the posts on the dock. Jagged edges below the neck of the bottle were as good as a knife as Michael rammed it into the guy's stomach. That was all it took. He saw a length of rope that the man had been using as a stringer and bound both of his wrists together, then threw his body out into the swamp at the end of the dock. That was the only kill he had any emotion over. Proud that he could help someone out in that way, but at the same time, hated having to kill him. He had been a believer. Maybe he shouldn't have done that, but he *had* wound up at the dock as if God had sent him there. If he hadn't, then the guy's death would've been a suicide instead of a murder and he would have gone to hell, so Michael stepped in and changed the course of his death. The guy was murdered, he didn't commit suicide.

It was a mercy killing. Michael tossed the whole bag full of unopened whiskey bottles in the lake away from the guy, and walked away.

It was all in a day's work. Not that he was trying to teach anyone a lesson, no. He just wanted to rid the world of the most uncaring and ungodly people in society and fulfill the mission he had been given. He wasn't worried about coming home with all of the blood on his clothes and washing it off under the water hose, and he wasn't afraid of leaving the knife, he had used to killed two people, at the scene of the crime. It's not that he was stupid, it's just that if this was his mission, then it would work out the way God meant for it to work out. He was confident. Killing them was not wrong. It was supposed to happen. Even if he got caught and put in jail he would get out. God would make a way. Tonight had been a new and exciting experience for him. The fact that he had worked as a tire tech for years no longer mattered. He had a new job now.

    He lay back in his cell on his cot and closed his eyes. Today, all of the people could rest, but tomorrow was another day. Another day closer to the day he would get out and kill again.

Mountain View

Chapter 3

Saturday morning Frank and Shelly got up with one agenda on their minds. Shopping. Today they would get all of their vacation equipment. They took turns in the shower. He read the morning paper while she was taking her shower, and she watched TV while she waited on him to finish his.

She went over to the desk and got the list of things they wrote out that they knew they had to have, folded it and put it in the back pocket of her jeans. It was a nice warm day out, this early in the spring, and she was ready to enjoy the weather and kick summer off. Today was only the 10th of April, but her favorite month of the year was just a little over two weeks away. Frank had finished getting ready and came out of the bathroom with a short sleeved polo shirt and a pair of jeans as well. Shelly was glad to see him in summer clothes again.

It was only 9AM when they walked out the door of their apartment, but they knew they would be gone all day. They got in their car and drove across town and out to Massachusetts. It took about three hours, which during that time, they talked about everything that had been going on with each other's jobs. They were always so busy with work that they seldom talked about it when they got home because they were too tired. Today they had time to talk and Shelly got to hear all about Frank's court cases and he was amazed to hear about all of the lives Shelly had helped transform through healthy eating and exercise. It was good to catch up and it reminded them of how impressed they each had been of the other's career when they had first met. They found a close parking spot at the Bass Pro Shop and started their exploration into the outdoors world of shopping.

The store had a huge stone fireplace as soon as you walked through the door, and taxidermy mounted animals of every description on all the walls, and the ceiling, and every nook and cranny. It was just like you'd stepped into the woods from the city sidewalk. The first thing they decided to look at was fishing poles, but realized it would be hard to get them on the plane, so they decided to get some once they were there. However, they did pick out a few things, like a small tackle box to carry in your pocket, and a stringer. Shelly thought they would be lucky if they actually caught a fish. It was rare that they ever went fishing. Living in the city like they did, there were so many other things to do, that they just never took the time to go and rent a boat and do that. They were unfamiliar with what bait to use for what fish and she was sure their casting technique needed a lot of work.

They went to the camping equipment and got a couple of rugged duffel bags, which would hold everything they ever needed on vacation, and then some. They both got new hiking boots and a few new pairs of shorts, t-shirts, and tank tops.

Harry had told Frank that the cabins were equipped with dishes and cookware, so they didn't need to buy anything like that. They would only have to buy the food that they wanted there, so that eliminated a lot of expense and excess packing. They had looked at the flashlights and lanterns, but had decided to wait and get them later at

Walmart or somewhere else, since they would be hard to carry. They had looked it up on the internet that there was actually a Walmart in Mountain View as well. They had giggled and said that there was no town in the United States that was really a town unless it had a Walmart.

They spent over two hours in the Bass Pro and had gotten everything they came for, and a few extras. They got a compass, some water bottles and some snack mix that they had never seen anywhere else. It looked too good to resist with the popcorn and peanuts mixed into the chocolate M&M's, and you can't really go camping without some beef jerky, so they got a small package of that too.

By the time they loaded their purchases into the car, they were exhausted and starving. Frank suggested that since it was almost 5PM, that they just stay there in Massachusetts and eat dinner, so they found a good hamburger joint and finished off a cheeseburger with fries and a Coke in record time. They stuck to their healthy diet most of the time, but at least once a week, they both splurged and ate whatever they wanted to. Shelly had been proud of Frank's diet change since they met, and they were both healthy and fit, so she didn't care to eat fattening food with him either. In fact, she secretly loved it, she just didn't want to blow her image to Frank. Frank took the time to exercise every other day, before or after work, depending on his case load or if he was due in court. On the weekend he would exercise longer. His exercise routine consisted of running for about a mile and then lifting weights, twenty five pound dumbbells with two "reps" each arm, 100 sit ups, and fifty push-ups. He never developed the muscular body of a drill sergeant, but was clearly in shape.

Shelly, on the other hand, did lots of different types of exercise all throughout the day, every day, with her clients. She took advantage of the time off and rested on the weekends. She was smaller in height and weight than Frank, but she was very toned and it was clear to see that she worked hard at keeping herself that way.

It was almost 10PM by the time they got back to their apartment and unloaded their car. It was a lot harder to get all their stuff up the stairs, than it was to buy it and put it in the car. They were tired and ready for bed. Tomorrow would be another day of shopping.

The next four weeks passed off quickly. Shelly wrapped up the session with her last client, and gave him instructions on what foods to eat and what not to eat. She reminded him of all of the exercises he should do, and reminded him to keep a log of his weight loss over the next month. She wrote her own progress report of that particular client down in her computer, and hit the save button and headed for home. This was Friday and they had tonight and tomorrow to pack before they would be getting on the plane for Mountain View Sunday. She was excited. She walked down the street to catch a cab home. While she waited, she called Frank on her cell. Frank was just finishing up at the office. He had had a busy week himself on several different cases, and was finishing up some of the last minute details with some of the clients. He was just about to walk out the door and start home too. Although they loved their jobs, it was nice to take a breather now and then and just have fun.

After a celebratory glass of wine with dinner and an hour of relaxing, they decided to take on the task of packing.

Shelly knew she would have more than Frank, so she got out her new duffel bag and her old luggage from when they got married. She also reminded Frank to pack their backpacks for when they went hiking. They both packed digital cameras which they would edit after their vacation was over. They would merge them together and put them on one disc and make their own "mini movie" to show everyone and be able to keep and watch over and over again in the years to come. They got the chargers and an extra micro SD card and batteries. They had gone to Walmart the day after they went to the Bass Pro and got their own First Aid supplies, and made a special bag for that and had packed it also. They had all the new clothes they bought for camping and some nicer clothing for going out. They had laptops, cell phones and all of the chargers for those also, plus plenty of money and credit cards, and last but not least, sunglasses. There was more than that stuffed into the extra backpacks as well.

    On Saturday they had rechecked and repacked their luggage until they were satisfied they had everything they needed. They both went and got haircuts and done last minute things like having the post office hold their mail. Now, on Sunday, they were loading up into the jet at LaGuardia that would take them to Wilcox Memorial Field in Mountain View, Arkansas. As far of a drive as it was, it would only take about two hours to fly there. There would be no jet lag on this flight. They let the baggage crew load their duffel bags, with Frank joking about Shelly packing everything but the kitchen sink, and they climbed aboard and buckled themselves in to the six seater jet, of which they were the only passengers.

"Not many people going to Mountain View, Arkansas today!" The pilot quipped.

Frank and Shelly laughed as they told him their story on how they picked their vacation spot. He seemed amused as he listened while also instructing them to buckle their seat belts and then pausing to radio the control tower for take-off.

****

In Tallulah, Louisiana, the jailer found a prison that would accept their serial killer inmate. It was in the northern part of Arkansas, far away from the delta, in a town called Calico Rock. He would be transported there within the next hour. It would be a long trip for the deputy that had to take him, six and a half hours to be exact, and he was programming it into his GPS. He grabbed a Coke and candy bar for the ride and put them in his patrol car. He let the prisoner, who had just had lunch, use the restroom before they left. He then escorted him out to the car, minus the shackles, but with a chained restraint belt. He put him in the back of the unit behind bars and Plexiglas. It would be evening by the time they got there, and way past midnight by the time the deputy got back. He got in the patrol car and put the hammer down.

As they flew down the two lane delta highway, the killer gazed out into the fields of soybeans and cotton passing by, and planned his escape. He didn't know the exact way it would happen or where it would happen. Only that it would.

****

It was almost noon when Frank and Shelly's jet landed in Mountain View. They had loved the view of the town and surrounding country from the air. To them, the town seemed so small, as they were flying over, after coming from a big city like New York, where they saw loops and whirls of concrete and asphalt roadways mixed with skyscrapers, here all they saw were mountains with a few roads scattered between them and the tiny town nestled in one small area right in a valley between some of the biggest mountains around.

They unloaded their bags and went inside the small terminal to ask about renting a vehicle, and to their surprise, there was no vehicle rental company in the whole town. "What are we going to do?" Shelly laughed and giggled at the same time. They couldn't believe it.

Frank thought a minute and decided to call Cecil and let him know they had arrived but didn't know how they were going to get to his cabins. After talking to him and telling him their predicament, Cecil said he would be glad to come out and pick them up and that it would be no trouble at all. True to his word, he was there in about twenty minutes and helped them put their bags into his 1970's model, square nosed GMC truck, red with a white stripe down the middle, and they took off for the "Hills and Hollers" cabins.

The airport had been located not far from the main part of town. On the way to the cabins they passed a few restaurants and the Walmart, and some antique stores as well. Cecil talked as he drove. He asked them how their flight was and what they thought of their town so far.

"It's small!" They both said in unison and Cecil

laughed.

"I figured you might think that. What is it ya'll do in New York?" He asked.

"I'm a criminal prosecutor, Frank answered, and Shelly is a fitness trainer."

"Well, those are both great things to be. Cecil stated. We don't have too much crime here in Mountain View, but we do have some. Drugs are everywhere, even here, and of course the usual drinking and fighting, but that's about it. Now as for the health of our population, I'd say a bunch of us around here might benefit from having a personal trainer!"

"Just too much good food!" Shelly said smiling.

"You betcha!" Cecil grinned. There's a lot of places here to eat and there's a variety of good stuff. We got pizza, cheeseburgers, Mexican, down home cookin, and even Chinese." Frank and Shelly told him that Chinese was one of their favorites.

"Since you're on vacation, you should try a little of all of it and see if there's anything you're missin." Cecil added. Frank and Shelly promised that they would and then jokingly added, as long as they didn't have to eat something like raccoon or possum. Cecil laughed out loud and told them that although the local restaurants didn't serve it, some folks around there still to this day might consider those two meats a delicacy. Frank and Shelly cringed at the thought.

They drove on past the main attractions and down through hills and valleys that were becoming more residential and country by the minute. They drove down a big hill that they could see other mountains looming ahead of them in the distance. The further down the hill they went, the bigger the mountains became. When they finally got to the bottom, the land leveled off for a ways, and they could see beautiful houses and scenery.

"That over there is the White River." Cecil said pointing to his right, as he pulled in the parking lot of "Fish-N-Dock". "There's good fishin there and good eatin, and if you go on down the road a little ways, there's another good fish house that I think you'll love. Right now, we're gonna go to the left here and I'll take you to our cabins."

They pulled back onto the highway and went back into a secluded road that wound and twisted its way back into the woods and ended at an open field that spread out at the foot of a mountain. The gravel road skirted the edge of the wood line and came to a small log cabin that served as an office. Outside, hanging from a post, was a carved wooden sign, that was painted with greens and blacks accented with purple, of mountains and valleys that said "Hills and Hollers Cabin Rentals" on it.

"Here we are!" Cecil said coming to a stop. He got out and walked around to Frank and Shelly and gestured for them to follow him into the office. There in the office was his family. His wife, a short, dainty looking woman with dark brown hair and big brown eyes, quite the opposite to Cecil's tall frame with his shock of salt and pepper hair, mostly salt, and white beard, greeted them with a big smile and a warm hello. The kids, all three, a boy and two girls, were almost the spitting image of their parents, each with different characteristics.

They looked to be from about ten years old, the girl being the youngest, to about fifteen years old and full of energy. They had been on the computer playing games when Frank, Shelly, and Cecil walked in. They all turned and politely said hello as well. It looked like they were all packed and ready to leave as all of their luggage was piled next to the couch on the other side of the room. Cecil introduced them and then confirmed that they were ready to leave on vacation themselves.

Escape

Chapter 4

The deputy and the killer had been riding for hours when they finally reached the town of Calico Rock. Interesting little place the deputy thought. The whole town was pretty much situated right on top of a bluff, and below the bluff, the White River circled the town and ran all the way from above Calico Rock, and eventually into the Mississippi River.

Calico Rock was an old town with old buildings that looked like they were still from the old west days of cowboys and Indians, and there was a railroad track that circled all the way around the town and crossed over a bridge that ran high over a gorge and was a beautiful scenic ride for tourists. Houses dotted the bluff all the way around the old town, some of them nice, three story homes that sat right on the edge of the bluff, looking down on the river and land below. The Calico Rock prison was a little ways out of the main town.

The killer wasn't noticing the town for its beauty, but for its escape route.

They finally made it to the prison where he could see the two sets of at least twelve foot high fences, with razor wire at the top. As they neared the main building, the concrete blocks the color of sandstone, the deputy pulled up in the circular drive and addressed the guard, who radioed for another officer to come down and escort them inside the walls.

The guard had just stepped back into his booth to log

in the deputy's patrol unit and the name and location in which he was from. The killer sat vigilant in the backseat, his muscles taut and his pulse racing, like a cat ready to pounce, just waiting for the right moment. While the gate guard was logging the information down, there was a van that pulled up with "Texarkana Regional Correctional Center" he could see written on the side, with six other prisoners, all dressed in white, in which the guard had to assist the driver and call for more officers to escort those prisoners.

The Madison Parish deputy got out of the patrol unit to lock his weapon in the trunk, as is standard procedure, since weapons are not allowed behind prison walls. The killer knew that if he got behind those walls, he would never get out. It was now or never and that's when he made his move.

A few hundred miles back, they had stopped at a rest area to use the restrooms. Six hours was too long for the deputy, who had eaten his candy bar and drank the Coke during the first hour of the trip, and he allowed the killer to relieve himself as well. As the prisoner was getting out of the patrol car, he noticed a defect in the way that the door of the patrol unit shut, where he sat in the back. The Nader bolt was bent downward to the point that the door didn't latch completely and he used that to his advantage. While he was using the restroom, the deputy stood slightly to the side of him to keep him within eyesight, but he noticed in the mirror that the deputy had turned his head to the side. While he wasn't looking, the killer grabbed the air freshener in the bottom of the urinal and broke off a flat piece of the plastic housing and hid it in his palm. Thanks to the deputy who had removed his chain restraint belt cuffs and used a pair of handcuffs instead, locking them in the front, so he could do his business without assistance. In fact, one hand was cuffed to a metal water pipe next to the urinal and the other was free. When he was done, the deputy put the other hand in the cuff that had been attached to the pipe, and walked him back out to the patrol unit. As he was getting in, he bent over as far as he could getting in the patrol unit and jammed the piece of plastic from the urinal freshener into the hole that the Nader bolt was supposed to fit into, as tightly as he could. He wasn't sure it would stay in place or be strong enough to keep the bolt from sliding in. As the deputy was shutting the door, he leaned his knee into it, as hard as he could without being obvious, to try and prevent it from closing hard all the way. The deputy shut the door without much force, turned and slowly sauntered back to the driver's door. As he was walking away, the killer leaned against the door and to his surprise, it gave way. He quickly shifted in his seat and with his right hand, pulled it to as good as he could get it, so that it didn't swing open while they were going down the road. He looked down on the door and saw a plastic panel that had a slight groove in it and he kicked off the orange government issued sandals, and dug a toenail into the groove to try to help hold it in place. He knew it wasn't a very good hold, but it was all he had because the door didn't have handles or armrests.

  Now, while the deputy was leaning over into the trunk of the patrol unit to secure his weapon, the killer made his move. He threw open the door, and barefooted, ran as fast as he could, across the prison yard, towards the nearest tree line, so that he might be able to take cover when they started shooting. He knew it was only a matter of seconds before that happened, and it did, but he had just enough jump on the deputy, who had already taken his gun off, and had laid it down in the trunk, that he was able to get to a slight ridge where he ran bent over, weaving right and left without getting hit. He knew they would be after him with dogs and guns and that the woods would be the first place they would look. He had on a bright orange suit and no shoes and was sure his scent would be easy to follow because he could feel his feet getting cut up with almost every step he took. The only advantage he had, was that it was getting dark. At least they wouldn't be able to see him as easy. His goal was to either find someplace to hide, which was unlikely, or to make it to the river. He figured the river was his best bet, and even that was going to be hard if not impossible. It was about a three mile drive from where he saw the river to the prison, but that was also around a curvy road. This way he was running directly toward it, which would make it a little closer. He was in great shape, since he was used to doing physically hard work on vehicles. He even ran regularly as a way to relieve stress, and so far, he hadn't even gotten winded.

It was almost dark when he reached a road. He knew he couldn't go down it because he would be seen for sure. He looked all around. In the very close distance he could hear the officers and the dogs as they trailed him through the woods. He only had seconds to make a decision. Suddenly, he heard a cow bawl over in the clearing across the road and had an idea. He ran across the road and over a small hill that was pastureland on the other side. He quickly crawled under the barbed wire fence and made his way towards the herd of cattle he saw grazing on some hay in a hay ring. Finding the loosely stitched hem at the bottom of the pant legs, he ripped the material upwards along the seam and then sideways as quickly as he could, tearing the legs off of his orange suit.

So as not to spook them, he quietly snuck up to the herd. The first cow that he came to was really a calf and much shorter than the full grown cows. He got right beside her and typing the legs of his orange suit together making a loop big enough that the fabric would touch the ground, he quickly threw the orange lasso over her head, slapped her on the side, and chased her as she took off running wildly, down through the pasture toward the barn. He sprinted a few feet backward and dove into the pile of hay inside the hay ring, digging his way toward the bottom, as close to the ground as he could get, making an air pocket to breathe into. He could hear the footfalls of the officers and the dogs barking as he lay there trying to catch his breath. He already made up his mind that if they found him, he wouldn't go down without a fight and had rather die by the hands of the officers than to go to prison for the rest of his life.

He lay totally still as they searched the area, the dogs yelping, uncertain, at first, of which way to go. He could hear the officers yelling to one another and on their radios. One of the dogs bayed loudly when it finally caught a strong scent of him.

"Looks like he snuck up on a cow and rode it bareback," he heard one of the officers yell, "The scent trail goes this way!"

"Let's go, let's go!" one of them hollered as they all took off in the direction of the calf. As soon as they were out of earshot, he crawled out of the hay ring and continued in the direction of the river.

It was pitch black outside now with only the stars for light. He could see an old house on a small hill up ahead. He really needed shoes. It wouldn't hurt to have some pants either since the majority of the bottom half of his were gone now. He got closer and crept up into the yard in the shadows. It was dark inside the house except for one room he could see a TV through the window. He carefully looked into the window and could see an old man sleeping on a couch, and an old woman asleep in a rocking chair. He went around the back of the house and tried the door. It opened. He snuck in quietly and quickly made his way down the hall. Looking for their bedroom, he found the laundry room instead: Clean clothes.

He dumped the whole basket on the floor and grabbed a pair of overalls and a pair of boots, not worrying about the size. He made his way back through the house and out the door. A few minutes later, the old woman woke up and went to the laundry room to get her slippers. She saw the laundry basket dumped all over the floor, and what appeared to be drops of blood. She stood there for a moment, and with a funny look on her face, scratched her head and shuffled back off to the TV.

The killer tried on the boots when he got back into the shadows and they were really too tight, maybe a half a size too small, but he could stand them for a little while. He had to have them to get anywhere. His feet were bleeding and he couldn't be in public without shoes. With the boots laced up and tied, he went out back to an old shed looking for some tools. Not finding any there, he went further, to an old barn and found exactly what he needed: a hacksaw. He worked quietly in the dark jamming the hacksaw in between an old engine block and an anvil, and raked the handcuff chain back and forth furiously, and with such force, the chain split in minutes. He would have to have something to pick the lock later though. He felt in the dark for a toolbox and found a nail and a file. He bound them together with some wire, and wired them to a loop on his suit, then took off again into the night. He finally made it to the edge of a high bluff. He could see the river below him. He finally found an area that more or less had a trail that would take him to the bottom.

When he reached the edge of the river he wondered how fast it flowed. It looked fairly slow when they had driven past it earlier. He stuck his hand in to feel how cold it was. Pretty cold since it was only May and had just been in the 80's for a couple of weeks. He decided to go for it. He was a swamp rat anyway, growing up on the banks of the Mississippi when he was a kid, and water had never hurt him before. Besides, if they did ever pick up his scent again, this would eliminate that problem.

He took off the boots and tied each boot to the loops on his suit, and tied his overalls around his waist. He eased in so he wouldn't make a splash, and sucked in his breath as the cold water shocked his body. He started to swim and eventually he became used to the numbing cold. At least it felt good to his feet.

Log Cabin

Chapter 5

Cecil asked them if they would like to go look at some of the cabins and have their pick of the one they wanted to stay in. He had ten in all, but there were five different styles that were repeated. They got back in the truck and drove to the other side of the open field, where another road went back into the woods and split off into five different directions. The first cabin was there about fifty yards back into the woods. It was a more contemporary style and had wood siding painted in a rustic red color and trimmed in white with solar lights lining the path. On down the road, about two tenths of a mile, the second one was more of a farmhouse style and actually looked like a barn, and had a small open field that surrounded it, complete with round hay bales and pitch forks and wheelbarrows. They went down another road behind it, in a different direction and the third cabin was a Victorian style cabin that was small but, had high pointed roofs and round tower rooms, and was loaded with window boxes all around. The fourth cabin was around a curve that snaked back behind the third cabin. It had a country style with the whole house made of rock and was accented by large bay windows in the front and a rock chimney. Last, the fifth cabin was backed up at the very foot of a huge mountain and was in perfect log cabin style. It had a tin roof and a porch that went all the way across the front of the cabin. The logs were "saddle notched" together with logs that overlap each other. There was also a rock chimney at one end of the cabin and even a dug well with a pulley and water bucket in the yard.

Cecil explained that these were all of the cabins on this side, and that the five other matching ones were on around from the first road they came in on, before they got to the office. The land on that side was more flat with no mountain behind it.

"You got your pick of any one you'd like to stay in. Which one would you like?" He asked.

Frank and Shelly glanced at each other, knowing which one it would be without even talking about it. Both of them wanted the same one, without question, and blurted it out immediately.

"We want this last one, the log cabin!" Shelly said excited.

Cecil laughed and said; "I figured you'd say that. Seems like this one is the most popular. I don't know what it is about it, whether it's the way it looks or that it's the most remote one of the bunch, but everyone wants the log cabin."

Frank and Shelly said it was a combination of the two and that it seemed so cozy and what they had always imagined for a vacation in the Ozarks. It just wouldn't seem right to stay in one of the others. Cecil agreed with them and said it was also his favorite.

He took them back up to the office to give them the keys. His family had loaded their stuff into a new, red Land Rover that was pulled up outside.

"Well, looks like my family is ready to go!" He laughed as he went inside and handed them the keys to that cabin. Then he handed them another set of keys. "I know you don't have a vehicle and I don't mind you using the truck out there. I'd like to ask you a favor. Since you are here while we're gone, I'd appreciate it if every morning and every evening you'd drive by all of the cabins and check on them to make sure no one has broken in and stolen anything, or staying there without paying. Also, check on the office to see that it hasn't been broken into. Everything is locked up, but that don't mean anything these days. The master key is on this key ring that the truck key is on, and it will open all of them, including yours. If you should have any trouble, he said handing them both a business card, here is the number to the police department, and we do have the 911 system in place here. Cell phone service isn't very good here, due to the mountains we're under, but each cabin has a phone and the office has one. The business number and address of this site is on the front of the card. If anyone wants to rent a cabin tell them they are unavailable due to maintenance for two weeks. I think that's about it!"

Frank and Shelly thanked him for the use of the truck and promised that they would keep an eye on the place. He told them to have fun and he would see them when they returned from the beach, but if they decided to leave before then, to give the keys to some friends of theirs at Hipp Modern Builders in town. Their number was also on the back of the card and their street address. Cecil assured them that the guy that ran and co-owned the place, Gentry Hipp, would know who they belonged to. Cecil was in there all the time for supplies for repairs on the cabins and he and Gentry were good friends.

With that last piece of information, Cecil said goodbye

and got into the car with his family. They all waved at Frank and Shelly as they drove off to start their own vacation. Frank and Shelly waved back, almost feeling like they were "kin folks", as Cecil would say, until they got out of sight and then turned to look at each other and said; "What do we do first?"

They decided to go back to their cabin and see what it looked like on the inside and unload their luggage and unpack it. They needed to see what kind of groceries or other supplies they might need as well.

It was fun going back down the road that went to the cabin they had chosen. They both giggled that the cabin was the first choice for both of them. They rolled the windows down on the truck with the hand crank handles, and just enjoyed the fresh air.

They pulled the truck up close to the cabin and began to unload their luggage, stacking it all on the porch. Then they opened the door and started bringing it in, placing it in the middle of the floor. The cabin was so beautiful. Built entirely of cedar, it had tongue and groove ceilings, and the walls were the actual logs it was built with. It had a small kitchen area with a bedroom beside it on the ground floor, and then the living room and dining area joined together off from the kitchen. On one wall there was a large bay window and on the other wall a rock fireplace with a bearskin rug on the floor below it and a stack of wood on an iron wood holder on the hearth. Above the living room were large cedar beams and an open vaulted ceiling going all the way to the roof. A set of stairs, along the far wall, led up to an open loft. Underneath the stairs was a tiny bathroom with a toilet and a small, one person shower. They both climbed the stairs to the loft, where underneath the sloped ceiling, was a full sized bed with a country handmade quilt, and a window behind the bed that looked out onto a field. The open space where they came up the stairs looked out over the living room and out some solid glass windows at the very peak of the roof. It was the most romantic place they had ever imagined. They decided that all of their nights on vacation would be spent in the loft bed upstairs. Frank laughed and told Shelly that if they weren't already married, he would propose to her right there on the spot. Shelly laughed out loud and gave him a kiss before she turned and headed back down the stairs to finish unpacking.

When they finally finished putting everything where it needed to go and made a list of the things they needed, they realized they were hungry, and they should've been, because it was almost five o'clock in the evening. They locked up their cabin and got in the truck to go in search of food. The grocery and supply list would have to wait.

They made it up out of the mountains they had been under and back to the main part of town. After eating, they went back to the Walmart they passed a couple of streets back. The first thing they noticed was it was not nearly as crowded as the one they went to in New York and the layout was different. It was, at least a "super center" though, and they would be able to get everything they needed.

They got some drinks and breakfast foods along with the normal stuff such as light bread and sandwich meats and the condiments to go with those. A can of coffee was a must, along with the late night snack supply of fruit bars. They also got a good book to read before they went to sleep at night. When they thought they had all they needed, they checked out, and was pleased that they had spent very little.

They decided to take a quick drive around town before they headed back. It would be a while before their groceries would spoil, and they wanted to take a better look than they had gotten to earlier with Cecil, since he didn't go on part of the main drag.

From Walmart they took a left turn and ended up at the intersection they came in on from the airport. They hung another left and went past a grocery store and a bank, and then saw some used furniture stores. On down from those on the left was a hardware store that said in big, bold letters "Hipp Modern Builders". They looked at each other grinning as they found the first landmark, which was the name of the business that was on Cecil's card he gave them to leave the keys with if they needed to.

They drove about five more minutes and decided to turn around, as town seemed to be running out. They got back to the intersection where they had taken the left turn and went straight on out. This was the part of town they had not seen yet. They passed by some gas stations, fast food restaurants, businesses, and churches and then they came to the old part of Mountain View.

Cecil had told them that Mountain View didn't exist until sometime around 1873, when a group of people had to decide what to name the county seat. The name "Mountain View" was submitted into a drawing and was chosen. He said that the county courthouse was built in 1890 out of logs and that businesses began to grow around it and then later on, a two story courthouse was built in 1888 and finally, a stone building was built in 1923 that's still there today.

Frank and Shelly enjoyed seeing the old stone buildings, which were two and sometimes three stories high, as they drove through town. Some of them now housed antique or clothing stores, and one was the town newspaper. They saw the sheriff's department in a red brick building, just off the main street, and then they saw the courthouse and the Court Square just a few yards down on Main Street. There were businesses all the way around the Court Square and restaurants on each side as well. There were bed and breakfasts behind the square in their own quaint little neighborhood. More antique stores, crafts, and music stores lined the streets. The courthouse itself was a large building of stone, which was mostly tan in color, with hints of red. It was on a large square patch of ground surrounded by a fence also made of stone, about hip high. In the center of the front of the building was a memorial to "Our Stone County Sons" of some of Mountain View's citizens that were in WWI. Next to the courthouse was an ironworks shop where they would fire and bend iron into tools or custom decorations. Just down from that was an old fashioned soda fountain with a pharmacy inside as well. After that, town pretty much ended and the rural farm country started in.

It was almost seven o'clock and they were both getting tired and knew they needed to get their groceries in the refrigerator and get back before dark and before they got lost, since they were not too familiar with the roads yet.

They headed back to the cabin and got there just at dusk.

As they were putting up their groceries, they marveled at the fixtures inside the cabin. Although they had equipped each place with modern utilities, there was an old red hand pump faucet for the kitchen sink that really worked, but the bathroom had modern fixtures in it. Frank was curious about the well outside and went to see if it was real. He lowered the bucket down on its rope until he felt it bump and then pulled it back up. It was full of cold water. He called to Shelly to come out and look. She did, and they laughed at the simpleness of it and ran back inside to get a glass to taste of the water. They were shocked at how much difference there was. No chlorine taste, and it was almost sweet. Although they both drank only filtered or bottled water, they thought that this was probably even healthier than those.

They went back inside and looked over their cabin some more. There was a nice large couch in the living room with its back to the kitchen so it would face the fireplace. The light above it was a metal sculpted frame with wildlife dancing all around the shade that threw shadows on the walls of deer and pine trees. Each light switch cover and power outlet were a hand carved pinecone design. On the walls were some mounted fish and deer. The little bathroom had the same pine cone decorations for the towel holder and toilet paper holder, and there was paneling with wildlife scenes as well. A magazine rack with current fish and game magazines hung on the wall.

It was only 9PM, but it had been a very long day, and Frank and Shelly were really tired. After looking over the downstairs, they decided to call it a night. They took what they needed upstairs to get ready for bed, each taking turns in the tiny bathroom so they hopefully wouldn't have to come back down.

They settled into their very comfortable pillow top bed with the country quilt, to read a chapter in the book they had bought, on hunting stories. The lamp by the bed looked like an old kerosene lamp but had been remade into a lamp with a light bulb. By the end of the first story, they were getting sleepy. Shelly switched off the lamp. The stars were bright outside the little window over the bed. Something they could never see in New York, and there were no noises of traffic or the honking of horns. All was peaceful except the sounds of their breathing. They said their goodnights and fell asleep in seconds.

From Calico Rock all the way to Mountain View, and other rural areas beyond, a massive man hunt was being conducted by each city police department, the county sheriff's departments, and they were even talking about bringing in the U.S. Marshalls if he was not found within the week.

There were countless warnings being played on each local news station and radio stations, warning citizens to be cautious of their surroundings and of strangers. They reminded them to lock their doors at night and the doors of their vehicles, and if they saw anything suspicious to alert authorities and not investigate it themselves.

They had shown his photo from the mug shot they had taken at the jail when he was arrested, and there was a full cover story on it in Mountain View's local paper. He was considered very dangerous, and although law enforcement didn't want to create panic, they knew the citizens needed to be informed.

Every time something like this happened, people tended to overreact to the point of ridiculousness and call in for every little thing. The last time someone had escaped from the county jail, one lady called in wanting an officer to come out to her residence because she believed she had him captured. She had created her own booby trap made from a galvanized wash tub, big enough to bury a 600 pound Sumo wrestler in, and she had hoisted it up off the ground from atop of her hay loft. Placing some food underneath it, figuring that the killer would be hungry, she had made a trip wire that worked it, and if he pulled on the ear of corn under it that the trip wire was attached to, the tub would come crashing down on top of him. The officer that went to investigate had his gun drawn as she pulled on the rope and raised the tub to reveal an old billy goat with an angry look on his face for being trapped underneath the tub, and a corn cob devoid of the kernels of corn with the cob itself almost completely eaten as well. The officer had never lived that call down, and to this day they still called him "billy".

Since the very first day they had broadcast it on the news, the calls to all the law enforcement agencies had doubled in number and had especially picked up throughout the night when people were supposed to be asleep.

He had swam for what seemed like miles. At first with an Olympic style of one arm up in the air, with his face down in the water, while kicking his feet like crazy, then when he began to tire, he would flip over on his back and swim that way with his broad arms in a sweeping motion, while steadily kicking with a slower, more relaxed rhythm. It was almost restful. Finally, he began to tire of both styles, and was about to look for a place to hold on the bank and rest when he saw it. He couldn't believe his good luck. There was an old style canoe tied to a piling of a dock. In fact, there were more on down from that one. He figured they must belong to a resort. No matter who they belonged to, he was taking one of them.

There was no way to get into a canoe while it was still in the water without tipping it over, unless it was shallow water. He swam up to it and the water was still chest high, so he walked it closer to the bank. It was tied with a slip knot at one end with an old rope. He quickly untied it and took the boots and the overalls off from around his waist, and put them in the hull and carefully stepped into it. The paddle was already in it. He dipped it into the water and quickly began to drift away.

He had been running on adrenalin since about 7PM that night and he had no idea what time it was, but it must be after midnight and he was starting to get very tired. And hungry! He hadn't eaten since lunchtime at the jail in Louisiana. He paddled for about another hour and decided he had gone as far as he could for the night. He needed rest and he had to get those cuffs off and the rest of the orange suit before he could go anywhere and be seen.

He paddled to the bank on the right side of the river and drug his canoe up out of the water. He wasn't sure if he would need it again or if it had a logo or was identifiable, in case they reported it stolen, so he dragged it up into the woods until it couldn't be seen from the river. He took his overalls out and wrung the water out of them and hung them on a tree branch to dry. The boots were hopeless. He put the little tools of nail and file, bound with wire, in the bottom of the canoe, and lay down right next to the canoe in the leaves, exhausted. Morning would come soon and he had to get going.

The first thing that woke him up was the sound of a crow cawing. He woke with a start, not remembering where he was at first, then it all came back. He sat up and ran his hands over his face feeling a thousand years old. The chains from the cuffs dangling past his wrist. "Time to get those off". He thought. He reached into the canoe and brought out the nail and file. With his right hand first, he tried sticking the nail into the key hole, but it wouldn't fit. Glad that he had grabbed the file, he put the nail down on a rock and began to file it down until he finally got it to fit in the hole. He had filed it almost flat and was able to turn the locking mechanism in the cuff enough that it sprang the lock, and he was rid of one cuff. The left one was even easier, and he took it off in seconds. He quickly stripped off the rest of the orange suit and put on the overalls. They fit pretty good. He found a rock that was big enough to hide the suit, after he dug out a small hole in the dirt underneath it, and placed it on top of the suit.

His feet were another story. They were worse than he had thought. He had several cuts and splinters, and his feet were red and swollen. He needed to find some alcohol or peroxide to soak them in before they got any worse, fast, but before he could do that, he needed some food. As much as he hated to do it, he knew he had no choice. He found an old dead log and rolled it over until he saw an earthworm wiggling back down into the dirt. He snatched up the worm before it went too far and quickly put it in his mouth, chewed it up, and swallowed it. He found more and ate until he wasn't starving. Eating worms wasn't as bad as he thought it would be, but it sure wasn't a gourmet meal either.

It was now time to move. He pulled the boots on over his sore feet. He didn't want to walk along the edge of the river for fear of being seen, so he went further back into the woods hoping that he would find an old store or somewhere he could get something for his feet.

Monday

Chapter 6

Frank and Shelly woke up with the sun shining softly through the little window above them. They had slept very soundly and felt rested and ready to start the day.

"What would you like to do today?" Frank asked her. "You want to hang around close to here today or go to one of the other towns?"

"I was thinking about hanging around here and maybe going up to those caverns and then maybe going hiking or swimming". She answered

"That sounds good to me. Frank agreed. "How about if we go hiking first and then when we get done, going to cool off in the cavern. It's supposed to be cool in there."

"You have a point!" She stated, her eyebrows raised and her lips puckered. Frank laughed at her funny face.

They got up, and decided to go somewhere and eat a big breakfast first before going hiking, but before they could do that, they had to keep their promise to Cecil and drive around and check all of the cabins and the office. A fruit bar split between the two of them would have to do until they were finished. They both had put on shorts and tank tops for the day with their new hiking boots. They grabbed their backpacks filled with water and snacks, and their cameras, and headed out the door to the truck.

As they made their rounds to each cabin and then the

office, Frank would get out and check the back door while Shelly checked the front door to each cabin. It only took them about forty five minutes to check all ten cabins and the office. Nothing seemed out of place and everything was locked up tight. When they finished, they were starving. They had remembered a little café, on Main Street close to the courthouse, which looked promising for breakfast, and decided to go there.

They parallel parked on the edge of the sidewalk and paid the meter. Walking hand in hand, they could smell the aroma of a country breakfast just yards away and picked up their pace. They walked in and found a booth amid the regulars and the vacationers. It was an easy choice for breakfast. Eggs and hash browns with gravy, bacon, toast and jelly and coffee. They even decided to split a side order of pancakes with hot maple syrup. When they got their order, they laughed at how much food they had and knew that hiking was the best thing they could do for themselves after such a meal, but while they ate, they decided it was well worth it.

After breakfast they drove back down toward their cabin to a place called Sylamore Creek. Frank had read in a brochure that there was a scenic hiking trail called The North Sylamore Trail that would be good exercise, plus give them a chance to take some photos.

They started out hiking at the base of a mountain that went through the woods, with the Sylamore Creek following alongside it. It was peaceful and quiet with only the leaves crunching with their steps. Pretty wildflowers, mushrooms and ferns were scattered here and there along the path next to rocks or downed trees and made great close up photos that would be beautiful as screen savers on their computers, or as photos for their apartment or their own home someday. They saw a beautiful waterfall and felt the mist of the water spray their skin and it felt good since they had worked up a sweat hiking. It was worthy of several photos and video as well. Then they came to some beautiful outcroppings of bluffs, a thing never seen in New York, and was awed at their composition of what kind of material they were made of, their structure and size, and the sheer simplicity of their beauty. Some had moss growing on them which just added to their character. They both remarked aloud "Who would think a rock could be beautiful?" But it was. The beauty didn't end there as they walked up the side of the mountain and along it's ridge and could see far off into the distance across the peaks and valleys of this Ozark land. They knew they weren't in the Grand Tetons or the Mountains of Colorado or Wyoming, but in this little known place of Mountain View, Arkansas, that was just as beautiful as any well-known national park in the U.S.A

Their hike finally came to an end around 2PM. They were thoroughly pleased at what they had seen. The weather was nice, but the temperature had gotten in the upper 80's and they were ready to go cool off and have a look at those caverns. They had already drank all of the water they had taken on the trail with them, so they bought some more at a gas station and munched on the trail mix they had opened on the last hour of their hike. Blanchard Springs Caverns was only about a twenty minute drive and being able to sit down and rest was good. They left their back packs locked up in Cecil's truck and took their cameras with them.

Back in East Carroll Parish, the deputy who had transported the killer to Calico Rock had finally gotten back to the Sheriff's office to fill out an incident report on what had happened. The Sheriff was on the phone to the local law enforcement in Calico Rock and the next neighboring town of Mountain View Arkansas.

"Is that right….The Sheriff said, rared back in his chair with one foot propped up on a file cabinet next to his desk. He did what?…Well you can't say he's stupid… Well, sir, I know him pretty well. We've picked him up several times before on assault charges and once for domestic abuse when he grabbed his girlfriend's arm too hard. Said he was trying to keep her from leaving. Always seemed like a pretty nice guy, besides getting mad at folks, but what I learned from some of the locals around here is he's had some bad luck lately. His mother just died about a year ago from cancer, and his dad ran off and left the family when he was a boy and he was the only one she had to take care of her. He had no other family here. He had never dated really, even as a young man. Neighbors said he had been dating a girl a while back and this was the first girl they had ever remembered seeing him with for any length of time. Anyway, the death of his mother affected him so, that she dumped him for another guy and he had been trying to get himself together and had started attending church but somewhere something went wrong and he got things messed up. The guys he works with said that lately he had been quoting scriptures and pretty much trying to "force" people to live like he thought they were supposed to according to God, and blamed their lack of sympathy towards other people and their carelessness or stupidity on why evil would happen to them. Yeah, so in other words, something snapped and HE started playing God." In the serial killer world, he would be known as a "visionary" serial killer. Yeah, he had been hearing voices, supposedly from God to kill these people. The Sheriff paused for a minute to listen and noticed the deputy had stopped writing to listen in on his conversation.

"His name....let's see, it's Michael Delacroix. Yes sir, I'm glad to be of help any way I can. You're welcome. Oh, and one more thing, he seems to be a disorganized type of serial killer in the way that he killed all those people. It didn't seem that there was any planning involved. There is absolutely no cleanup of the crime scene or disposal of any evidence. There are shoe prints everywhere, bloody fingerprints, all his I'm assuming, and everything. No trying to dispose of the bodies. Seems he's just going off of adrenaline. Yes. Well, crazy is crazy. You just never know what they'll do. There's not always a rhyme or a reason, except to them in their own mind, and you have to be able to think like them to catch them and that's hard to do. Ya'll just be careful....he's dangerous." With that the Sheriff hung up the phone and turned to the deputy.

"What happened wasn't your fault, so don't think you did something wrong, okay. He said to the deputy. Things just happen. Just glad you didn't get hurt or killed. That will teach us all a lesson in safety and our own equipment. Go ahead and finish your report. Word it well."

With that he walked out of the room with a loud sigh to

go face the reporter who had been trying to get a statement from him for two days about what happened.

Michael Delacroix had walked and walked with every step feeling like his feet would literally burst open they hurt so bad. He had to get something to make them feel better, and he needed to get some more shoes. He thought that soon he would surely reach civilization of some sort.

It was probably close to noon the way the sun looked in the sky, and he had been walking for at least two hours or more. The woods seemed to be getting a little less thick and he thought he could make out a clearing up ahead. The closer he got, he could also make out the roof of a house. Excited, but cautious, he crept up on it slowly and quietly. It was a log cabin. There were no vehicles parked out front and he had sat and watched the house, looking inside the only window he could see into, and there appeared to be no activity. He made his way closer and inched around the side of the house and looked around the corner to the front porch to see if there were any dogs that would give away his presence. As soon as he saw there weren't any, he slowly walked upon the front porch and peeped into a window. It was dark and quiet. He could see a few things scattered around and knew that someone stayed there, but apparently they were not there now. He had to act fast. Proud that he had kept the tools he had stolen to take off the cuffs, he again dug them out of his pocket and with skill, opened the front door and stepped inside. By the looks of the place he could tell that this was not a home that was lived in, but a rental or resort cabin. There was only a small amount of property that belonged to someone and he wasn't certain what he would find to use.

He knew that his feet were the first priority. He searched through the tiny bathroom and found nothing. He noticed the loft upstairs and climbed the stairs two at a time.

He hit pay dirt when he found the duffel bags that contained a large first aid kit with antiseptics and antibiotic cream. He didn't want to tip anyone off that their stuff had been stolen and have them go reporting it, so instead of taking the whole first aid kit, he carefully took only one of each thing but several of some pain relievers, and stuffed it back in the duffel bag.

He ran down to the kitchen and found some empty water bottles and filled them half full of the peroxide and alcohol he had found as well. He returned back to the kitchen and found a plastic bag to carry his loot in. Before he left, he had to have some food. He opened up the refrigerator and smiled. There was lunch meat and cheese with soft drinks and bottled water. He quickly made himself a double decker sandwich with extra meat and cheese and stuffed it in the bag. He grabbed a soft drink, since there were more of them than there were water bottles, and filled another empty bottle he had found with tap water from the hand pump in the sink. He knew he had to get out soon and he grabbed a few loose snacks he knew they wouldn't miss and turned to leave. Just as he was going out the door that he had just turned the lock on, he noticed a pair of tennis shoes next to a chair. He grabbed one and tried it on and it was a perfect fit. He stood there thinking. He needed the shoes but knew that it would really be noticeable. He finally decided to leave them there and hoped that when his feet healed a little that he could tasks, stand the old boots until he could find some other shoes or get his hands on some money to buy some. He was amazed that in his search through their belongings, that he didn't find any money or credit cards. People usually didn't want to carry their whole stash with them when they went out, but either they hid it well or they had taken it with them. He would've taken only a small amount anyway, but anything would have helped.

    He had closed the door and made sure it was locked and started walking through the woods again, but close enough to the edge that he could follow the gravel road that he assumed would lead to more cabins and eventually to the main road. He needed some place to hang out for a couple of days until his feet healed and until he could figure out what he was going to do or where he was going. He couldn't believe his good luck. At least now, he had something to eat and his stomach was growling in anticipation of his next meal. He walked as fast as he could until he saw the next driveway veering off into the woods.

    The next cabin he came to was the Country Rock cabin and, like he done before, he made sure no one was home. He could clearly tell that no one at all occupied that cabin and there would be no cash on the premises to steal. He sat down on the porch to eat the sandwich and drink the water. He couldn't ever remember a time that bologna tasted so good. He sat there thinking that if there was someone that occupied the first place he came to, then someone would possibly be renting this one or, at the least, checking on it. He wondered how many more cabins there were and where the office was. That would be a long walk just to find out and the day was half over. He figured that since no one had already rented this one, that it might possibly be safe to hole up here tonight and check out the situation in the morning and be out before anyone could rent it. Satisfied that he had made the best decision, he waited until almost dark, then picked the lock and went inside to take a shower and see if there was anything useful.

Mindful not to get anything dirty or turn on the lights when it did get dark, he finished showering and shaved with the complimentary razor and bar of soap. He added those to his pack of stuff. He had only worn the clothes since morning, but after walking for at least a mile through the woods and brush, decided to go ahead and wash and dry them. While they were in the dryer, he tended to his feet. He knew it was going to hurt, but it had to be done. He picked out briars and splinters earlier and could see the festering sores from last night's run. He sat down on the edge of the bathtub and poured peroxide over each foot. That wasn't so bad, but then came the alcohol. It was all he could do not to yell. He gritted his teeth and kept pouring. After the torture, he carefully dried them off on a paper towel which he flushed down the toilet afterward, and rubbed antibacterial gel on them, and then wrapped them in gauze. He hoped this would take care of the soreness and prevent any further infection. He would do it again the next evening.

After his clothing came out of the dryer, he put them back on in case he needed a fast getaway, and looked for an exit route besides the front door. There was a back door in the kitchen. Now that he had finished all the really important

he decided to prowl around in the cabin and see what else he could find.

It was about to get dark and he had found a phone book that said Mountain View, Arkansas. He at least knew where he was. He thumbed through it getting bits of information and saw a small map that gave him an idea how big the town was. The size of the phone book told him that it wasn't a major city. He looked up all of the cabin rentals and tried to figure out which one he was at and then had the idea to look around the cabin for stationery or ink pens or pencils with the name on it and sure enough he found some in a kitchen drawer underneath the telephone. He smiled at the name "Hills and Hollers" and thought to himself, "Yeah, that's about right". He saw that he was on the far end of town and there were several more "hills and hollers" he would have to climb out of if he didn't find some other means of transportation.

It finally got so dark he couldn't see, so he put the phone book back where he found it and made a search of the fridge and cabinets to see if there was any more food. He lucked out and found some crackers and peanut butter in individual cups and there was some flour that someone had left over. He found a bowl and stirred up some biscuits with flour and water and put them in the oven. No one would be able to tell he was cooking that. When they were done he feasted on hot biscuits loaded with peanut butter and the soft drink he had gotten at the last cabin. He ate until he was stuffed.

He made sure the front door was locked and placed a stack of pans in front of it to wake him if someone came in. The sack of first aid supplies he left next to the back door with his boots. Tomorrow would be a busy day and he needed to get an early start. There was an alarm clock in one of the bedrooms and he brought it into the hallway and set the alarm for 5AM That should give him enough time to get himself together and clean up and get out before anyone came. He took a pillow off of the couch and a quilt he had found on the end of a bed, and lay down on the floor out of sight from the window, and fell asleep almost as soon as his head hit the pillow.

Frank and Shelly had a wonderful time at Blanchard Springs Caverns. There were three different tours they could have gone on, but they chose the Dripstone Trail, which was a shorter trail and sounded the most interesting. They learned that the cavern had three levels and had started forming over 350 million years ago. The temperature felt good to them when they entered, at a constant fifty eight degrees year round, but they were shivering by the time they got out!

They were amazed at the beautiful formations of large stalactites and stalagmites formed from mineral deposits that build up over the years, from constant drops of water. There were some that looked like drinking straws hanging down or sticking up, and some that hung in strips and looked almost exactly like bacon. There was even a Cathedral Room, which was more than 1,000 feet long and had a stone column that was more than six stories tall. They took some photos of many of the formations and of all of the rooms and the underwater river that flowed through the cavern. They couldn't wait to show them to all of their friends and family. There was one area where people had created their own "wishing well" and had thrown countless amounts of change in and made a wish. The tour guide said that they collected it once a year and usually got several hundred dollars each time.

It was almost 5PM by the time they got out of the cavern and they were getting hungry. They really wanted to eat before it got any later and decided they would check all of the cabins after they got back.

This time they decided to go for something different. They wanted to try catfish. There was a place they had passed that looked like a good restaurant and it was just down the road from their cabin. It was situated right on the edge of the White River and had looked full every time they passed by.

They drove down the hill beneath a large bluff and parked the truck in one of the only spots left and walked in. They were seated at a table that sat right against large glass windows overlooking the river. They both ordered catfish with pinto beans, pickled tomatoes, French fries, and hush puppies, topped off with sweet iced tea. They inhaled their meal and enjoyed every bite. Full and happy, they left a nice tip and headed back to the truck. Now they just had to make their rounds before they got back to their own cabin for the evening.

They pulled up to the office and each took their turns of checking the front and the back. Everything was locked up tight and they went on to do the cabins. The Contemporary and then the Barn cabin, followed by the Victorian. Next came the Country Rock cabin and they went a little quicker at it, due to the fact that it was so much darker in that area and they had meant to get flashlights at Walmart but had forgotten them. There was barely any light showing on the front porch and no light at all in the back and the house was dark inside, as it should be. Both doors were locked and nothing seemed out of order. The last cabin was their own and they were ready to get to it. What they didn't know was that inside that last cabin, a serial killer lay soundly sleeping and snoring so loud that he never heard them pull up in the truck or never heard the rattle of the door knobs as they checked to see if it was secure. Neither would be the wiser in the morning for the near miss.

When they got to their cabin, they were exhausted from the day's events. They each took turns at the shower and then went upstairs to the loft to go to bed.

"I love those new hiking boots I got!" Shelly said to Frank smiling as she dried off her hair with a towel.

"I really like mine too, but I seem to have worn a blister on my toe from breaking them in." He answered.

"I brought some antibiotic gel in the first aid kit." Let me get it. Shelly said digging in her duffel bag for it. She brought out the red, white, and blue canvas bag and found the zippered compartment that she had put it in. "Hmmm...I thought I brought more than that." She said with a puzzled look, but shaking her head. Knowing her, she had probably misplaced it before she put it in the bag. She handed it to Frank with a Band-Aid and crawled into bed next to him.

"What's up for tomorrow?" She asked.

"Do you feel up to canoeing on the White River?"

"Sounds fun to me!" She beamed.

"Okay, then. Let's get some sleep and we'll get an early start tomorrow and pack a lunch and go.

I put the camera batteries on the charger and the cell phones while you were taking a shower, so they'll be charged."

"Aren't you sweet!" She giggled as he leaned over and kissed her goodnight.

Tuesday

Chapter 7

Beep...beep...beep...beep...Michael Delacroix awoke with a start to the sound of the alarm clock in the hallway. He looked around and crawled across the floor to shut it off. It was still dark out, but the sun would be up soon. He turned on the oven again and went to relieve himself while it was heating up. As he walked he could tell that his feet felt a lot better than they did the day before. Some of the soreness was gone.

He went to the kitchen and stirred up some more biscuits, his new found gourmet breakfast, and put them in the oven. Then he sat down on the toilet in the bathroom and unwrapped his feet. They did look better, but he wiped off all of the gel and put on a fresh new coat. He dreaded putting the boots on, especially without socks but he had to. They didn't feel good, but not as bad as before.

As soon as the biscuits were done, he gave them a heavy coating of peanut butter and ate them quickly with some water. He knew it was silly, but wished he had some jelly to go with it. Water was all he had to drink now and the peanut butter would be gone soon. He had to find more food. He made a few extra biscuits and smeared them lightly with the peanut butter and wrapped them in plastic wrap and put them in his sack in case he didn't get a chance to make it back to the cabin. He put the blanket back on the bed and the clock back on the nightstand and made sure everything was as it were before he arrived, then he slipped out the back door locking it as he left.

He started walking down the gravel road ever mindful of any noise that sounded like a vehicle coming. He would see three more empty cabins before he finally got to the office at the end. He was puzzled when he got there. No one was there. It was already past 8am, according to the alarm clock he saw at the last cabin he had picked the lock on. Someone should be there around the clock or at least during business hours. He wondered where they were. He decided to sit back in the woods for a while and watch to see if anyone ever showed up. If not, he would made his move to go inside.

He sat there, for what he thought was probably an hour, listening and thinking when he heard a vehicle in the distance to his right. It was coming from the cabin side. As it slowly pulled up to the office, he could see that it was occupied by a man and a woman who looked like they were in their twenties. It must be the ones who were staying at the first cabin he had come to yesterday. They got out of the truck and went to the door and tried the knob then walked all the way around it. It was strange that they were the only ones there renting a cabin and that the office was empty and closed up. He wondered if they were the owners but dismissed that idea because of the material he had seen in their cabin. Were they trying to get in or just checking the lock? And if they were just checking the lock, then what were they doing that for if they weren't the owners and the owners were gone? Maybe they were also staying there without paying and trying to break in? He watched them get in their truck and drive away. He didn't know what the deal was with that, but he figured that he might have a limited amount of time to see if he could get in himself, so he ran from his hiding place and onto the porch with his tools.

First he tried the bottom door knob lock and it seemed to unlock, but this time there was an additional lock above that, a deadbolt, that wouldn't budge. He went around back, but there was no back door to the office. He peered in the window. He could see that the computer was turned off and a message light blinked on the phone. It looked like no one had been there at least overnight to check the messages. What was he going to do now?

He sat down on the porch railing to think. He needed more food. He needed money. He needed shoes and he needed a way out of here besides on foot. If he had some better shoes he could walk farther, but even that wouldn't be helpful enough to get out of those mountains quickly. It would take him days and they would be looking for him. Every day they would think he went farther and farther. It might be a good idea to actually hang out here a little longer since all of the cabins were empty except the last one. Maybe he could "borrow" a few more items from them while they were gone.

Still feeling full from the night before, Frank and Shelly skipped breakfast and both laughed at how much food they'd been eating and how fat they would get if they kept eating like this. Shelly said she could tell she had already gained a couple of pounds and they had only been there for two days! Frank said he felt heavier as well.

Canoeing would take some of that weight off because they were going to paddle for several miles and burn it off.

Swimming, they realized, was out of the question because it was still too cold here in the Ozarks to swim. They planned to work hard paddling and rowing. Frank had also remembered to take their camera batteries off the charger and they looked forward to taking photos of the sites they would see.

Frank had noticed a sign at the bottom of the mountain where the road to the cabin resort they were at and the main highway intersected that advertised where you could rent a canoe and fishing equipment. He saved the number in his phone and called them to ask for directions. Within minutes they were there getting a map of where they would be canoeing and getting assigned a guide.

Decked out with life vests, paddles and all of the necessary gear, they started off down the wide, and lazy river. They immediately went under a large steel bridge way above the river which was their first photo. The next was of a white house with a red roof that was at least three stories high perched on the top of a mountain overlooking the land below and the river. It was beautiful. They knew that the owners must love the view and had the right idea for where they built it.

They saw more beautiful houses and cabin rentals on each side of the river for a long ways, with mountains on all sides. It was so relaxing. After taking several photos, they picked up the pace again to burn some calories.

They paddled with a fast and steady rhythm for at least a couple of miles before slowing down to catch their breath and get a drink. They had worked up a sweat and it felt good. It had been a little cool when they first started out, especially in shorts, but now they were glad to have them on. There were other people in canoes as well and they had chatted as they slowly paddled by. Everyone was friendly and having a good time.

After resting, they picked up the pace again and passed everyone they had met. They were all laughing at them as they sailed by at Frank and Shelly's "competition like" speed. They had both called out that they were "burning off breakfast" and laughed as they paddled. Just after 1PM they finally came to a stopping spot where a bunch of other canoes had also docked and they got out with their food and water and took a break to stretch their legs and walk around. Everyone talked and visited and told where they were from, with Frank and Shelly coming from the farthest distance. They answered lots of questions about what New York was like and they learned a lot about why people were here from other states. Some of them stated that they just enjoyed nature and seeing it in new parts of the country. Others said it was the perfect way to spend time with the family that didn't cost an arm and a leg, with the way the economy was going, it was the most economical vacation they could afford and enjoy. They all thought it was a cute reason that Frank and Shelly chose Mountain View to get away from the city and go somewhere really country. Not all of the people canoeing were from far away, some were locals and told Frank and Shelly that if they really wanted to have a good time, they should come back in October when the "Bean Fest" was held on the Court Square. It was a festival held, where thousands of people came and contestants who entered would cook pinto beans in large black kettles around the courthouse square.

Everybody there could have free beans and cornbread for lunch and the judges would pick a winner. After lunch they had outhouse races where different teams from Arkansas and other states would push outhouses built on wheels and race each other. The winner would get a gold painted toilet seat with their name engraved on a metal plate, attached to the toilet seat, as a trophy. It was funny and everyone had a good time at the fest.

Frank and Shelly enjoyed all of the stories and thought the festival would have been the neatest thing they could ever have attended. They decided to keep it in mind and possibly fly back just to go to it in the fall. They shoved off again after thanking everyone, shaking hands, and getting a couple of e-mail addresses. They had made some new friends.

They had left Cecil's truck back at the restaurant and they finally made it to the destination where they met the guide who would take them back to the truck. It had been a fun ride, but they were ready to get out of the boat and walk for a while.

It was 3PM and they decided to go back to their cabin and change clothes and clean up so they could go out and eat later. They didn't expect what was coming next.

****

Michael Delacroix sat on the porch rail thinking for a while. He knew he needed the truck, but he really had no way of getting it. Hot wiring it was not an option, because he didn't really have any tools to do that. Plus, he didn't want to kill them just to get it, because then the cops would find out and know where he had been and what he was driving.

He needed a clean getaway. Besides, he didn't kill just anybody for no reason at all. The others he had killed had been shown to him that they were "chosen" and, sure enough, when he approached them they were not God fearing people. So far, he had not heard the voice tell him to do that with the couple driving the truck and staying in the last cabin. But if he ever did, he would have to kill them. They seemed like a nice couple but he really needed their truck.

With his stomach growling, he thought that since he had happened upon the leftover peanut butter and crackers, that some of the other cabins might have leftovers as well. There was a sign outside the office that showed a small map that listed ten cabins, and so far, Michael Delacroix had only seen five. There must be another road that was past the cabin going out towards the highway. If he didn't find food or money on this side, he might find it on the other side. Might even find someone else staying there that had a vehicle and needed killing. He reminded himself again that he needed to hold off on the killing as long as he could.

He hated what his life had become. He used to have it all figured out, or so he thought, until his mother got sick and died. After that, things started to fall apart. He had tried to do the right thing, and it seemed to go okay for a while, but then his girlfriend left him when God gave him his mission. He tried to get her to understand how he felt and that certain people shouldn't be allowed to live. She had cried and begged him to realize that God didn't appoint someone to do his job. God would do it himself. He had argued with her and scared her. She had packed up all of her clothes right after their argument that night and was walking out to her car to leave when he grabbed her arm. She had screamed and a neighbor heard her and had called 911. He should've killed her first, but just as he was making that first decision with his hand still clenched around her wrist, the Sheriff's department pulled up and arrested him for domestic abuse. He had grabbed her so tightly, there were bruises on her arm.

If killing ungodly, selfish people was what he was supposed to do, he was sure doing it now. At first he was confused. He knew the scripture said; "vengeance is mine saith the Lord". But he knew it also said "an eye for an eye". It felt like when he begged them for help and asked them to pray with him and they didn't, that this was his answer. Therefore, he felt that it was his duty to kill them.

It was already about noon. If he was going to have time to search more cabins he would need to create a diversion to keep the couple with the truck busy so they wouldn't be making their rounds too many times and he would have more time to look. He would try to make it look like "an act of God" he thought as he laughed to himself, and what better place to start than at their own cabin.

He quickly ran, stopping to rest only a couple of times, until he got to it. He picked the lock and went in. It would have to be something bad enough they had to fix now. He went straight to the bathroom to look at the plumbing. Of course the toilet was secured to the floor with no pipes showing, and the shower was also, but the sink was attached to the wall with a small enclosed cabinet below it. He opened the cabinet doors and saw PVC pipe. That was something he could work with. He then went to the kitchen to see if he could find a box of matches.

He carefully searched through the drawers until he not only found matches, but a grill lighter as well. He looked through the utensils and found tongs that would be useful and a rubber oven mitt. He took these items back to the bathroom and sat down on the floor. He got the piece of wire he used to pick locks out of his plastic bag and put it between his lips. He put on the rubber mitt and transferred the wire to it and lit the lighter. He held it in the flame until the wire glowed red hot, then he quickly grabbed the tongs and pinched them up close to the red hot end and stuck it right to the pvc pipe where the water should flow in from outside. It took a few tries but he finally got it melted enough that a thin stream of water began to spray out. He had put the hole right where two pipes connected and hoped it looked natural. He wiped off any black residue and got some fine dirt from outside to wipe around the pipe so it didn't look too clean.

He wanted it to look like it had happened early in the morning, so he took all the utensils back to the kitchen first and put them up, then filled a large bowl with water and poured it on the bathroom floor. Then about three more. By the time he had finished, the bathroom floor was covered and the water had ran out into the living room and snaked across the hardwood floor under a large area rug in the middle of the room. He dried and put the bowl back up and smiled at the job he had done. This should keep them busy for a little while.

He took another look around the house to see if they had left anything lying around. Still no money or anything. He went back to the kitchen and grabbed another Coke and made another sandwich and stuffed them in his plastic bag. He would eat good again tonight.

He locked the front door as he went out and started back up the road. He was going to try the Barn Cabin out tonight and see if it had any food.

He could hear a vehicle coming fast. He ran off into the edge of the woods and dropped to the ground behind a big oak. It was the couple in their truck. They had come back early. He was lucky he had gotten out just in time.

Frank and Shelly were ready to come in and get cleaned up, but when they walked through the door, they couldn't believe it. Water was everywhere. They followed the source and saw it running out from the bathroom cabinet. When Frank opened the doors, water shot out from the hole and sprayed him in the face. The pipes were fitted with shut off valves, so Frank turned one and sure enough, the spray stopped, but that would also shut off the water on the shower too wouldn't it? He had Shelly go turn on the shower and it came on. Luckily it was hooked up separately.

"What are we going to do?" Shelly asked.

Frank thought for a moment and said that the best thing they could do would be to take photos of it with their cell phone to show Cecil. Then go up to, "Hipp Modern Builders" and show them. Maybe they could help them get the right materials and give them advice on how to fix it. It shouldn't be that hard, and they would pay for the materials and Cecil could reimburse them.

After taking pictures, they decided to move the living room furniture and carry the large area rug outside to dry. The heavy cedar couch and chair was hard to move. They picked up the rug and carried it out first and threw it over the porch rail to drip dry. Water poured out of it. Then they got towels and soaked up what they could on the living room floor. The bathroom would have to wait. They threw the wet towels in the washing machine to wash while they were gone.

They found their way back to "Hipp Modern Builders" and parked in front of the large metal building. Shelly had reminded Frank to ask for the guy that Cecil told them was his friend. They walked down the center main isle of the store, up to the desk and asked to speak to Gentry. The employee they asked simply turned around and tapped another guy on the shoulder behind him that was on the phone. He was hanging up as he turned around. "They asked for Gentry." The employee told him.

"I'm Gentry. What can I help you with?"

Gentry was a young guy still in his twenties, probably close to Frank and Shelly's age. He had short brown hair with hazel green eyes and a goatee, and was wearing a Hipp Modern Builder's t-shirt in bright royal blue. He smiled from ear to ear like a country gentleman when Frank told him their story and explained about Cecil and then the water leak.

"Well, let's go over here and see what you're gonna need." Gentry said walking them down an isle in the store.

Frank explained to him where exactly it was leaking

and helped him determine the right size of pvc pipe. Then he got them a hacksaw, and new rings just in case. Gentry also suggested some plumbers putty to seal it up tight.

Shelly asked if there were any mops in the store so they could get all the water up out of the floor. Gentry suggested a large sponge if the floor wasn't too big, and a plastic bucket to go with it.

"Another thing we keep meaning to get is a flashlight or two. Frank stated. Do you have any of those?"

"I think we might have two or three of them." Gentry said, taking them down through the maze of isles that held everything from hardware merchandise like table saws, and tape measures, to mixing bowls and hand towels.

Frank picked out a slim aluminum flashlight to carry in his pocket and Shelly picked out a smaller, but just as bright, LED flashlight for herself, then they took their stuff up front to pay. There was an ice chest full of different kinds of soft drinks with unusual flavors that you didn't see in most convenience stores. Gentry told them it was a promotional thing he bought at a hardware convention and gave each of them one to go "on the house".

Frank paid for their stuff and thanked Gentry for helping them. Gentry told them to give him a "holler" if he needed anything else. He also gave them his cell phone number after they explained that Cecil said to leave the keys with him if they had to leave early.

"He was a pretty cool guy." Frank said to Shelly as they were on their way back to the cabin.

"Yeah, people here are really friendly. Shelly answered turning to look at him. They actually seem to have time for you and act like they care."

"Big difference from New York, huh?" Frank mused with a laugh. Not that there weren't nice people there in New York, but everyone was in a hurry and saw so many people and were so busy, that they tended to have an attitude at times.

They got back to the cabin and took all of their supplies in. Shelly mopped up the water with the sponge and bucket while Frank threw their load of towels they had in the washer, into the dryer. It only took a few minutes to soak up what water was in the floor.

Even though the pieces were plastic, Frank was glad he had gone ahead and gotten a pipe wrench, because they were on there tight. He got the pieces taken apart and put the new ones on, sealing around the threads where they fit together with the plumbers putty. The whole thing only took a matter of minutes.

In the time they were gone and got back, it gave Michael Delacroix time to search the Barn Cabin for some food, and to make sure it was a safe place to hide for the night. As he took a look around, he didn't see any reason it wouldn't be as safe as the first place. No one was there and there was a front and back entrance. Just like the other two places before, it was easy to pick the lock.

****

It was past 5PM when they finished their repair and Frank and Shelly were starving. No time to waste on cleaning up and looking good. They jumped in the truck and off they went.

"O.K., the first night we had burgers, the next night it was fried catfish. How about something not quite as fattening?" Shelly asked.

"I saw a Chinese place not far from here!" Frank said.

"That sounds great. I was kinda missing some of our usual stuff." Shelly smiled.

"Yeah, me too. Frank agreed. Funny to imagine one way out here, but I'm glad they have one."

Shelly laughed thinking about it and said; "If it was a culture shock for us just coming from New York, think what it must be like coming from China to live here!"

They parked a few spaces away from the door as the parking lot was quite full, which meant that it must be good if they had lots of customers. They could hear the soft chimes and flutes of Chinese music as they opened the door and stepped in.

After not having eaten Chinese for several days, it was easy to pick what they wanted. Shelly ordered the seafood vegetable delight and Frank had shrimp with brown sauce. They also had a bowl of egg drop soup. Just as they finished the soup, two sizzling plates of food with bowls of rice were set down before them and they ate until they were nearly sick. The Chinese food here was even better than from New York. When they paid, they got their fortune cookies at the register and took them out to the truck before opening them.

"Hmm…Frank said with a frown. Not sure I like mine."

"What does it say?" Shelly asked looking over at him.

"Be wary of your surroundings. Danger lurks." He answered.

"Gosh! Shelly exclaimed. Hope mine's better!" She said opening hers to read it.

"A new adventure lies ahead. One you won't likely forget."

"Better than mine!" Frank stated as he turned the ignition in the truck and it started with a loud rumble of the exhaust pipe as he revved the motor just for show. They felt like teenagers out on the town. They pulled out of the parking lot and headed back to the cabin. It was only a little after 7PM, but they were exhausted. Shelly took a hot shower first, then Frank, and they went upstairs to bed. They read one story in their book and fell asleep almost before the light was out.

Wednesday

Chapter 8

Michael Delacroix had hit the jackpot of food items. At the Barn Cabin there were a couple of cans of Pork-n-Beans and a can of chili that someone had left. There was also a box of stale crackers that would be just fine, and for dessert, a bag of marshmallows. There were no soft drinks, only water, but he did find a couple of packets of instant coffee.

After all the work he had done, and walking, he was tired and hungry. At 6PM he decided to eat. He washed his hands with dishwashing liquid and opened a can of Pork-n-Beans. After he heated them on the stove, he crumbled crackers in a bowl, and had a feast. For dessert, he popped a couple of marshmallows in his mouth. He took a quick shower and washed his clothing again, always listening for the sound of intruders. He had waited on the couple in the truck to make their rounds, but they hadn't yet and it was late. He would wait until well after dark to go to sleep just in case.

He put the rest of the food in his sack like before, in case he had to leave, and had found a place to sleep in between the front and back door, out of sight. He would need to think about leaving soon.

He had checked his feet again after he showered and they were almost well. He still kept putting medication on them. Deciding that his getaway might be easier if he trimmed his hair, he gave himself a very short haircut with a pair of scissors he found in a kitchen drawer and he flushed the hair down the toilet.

Finally about 9PM he decided to go to sleep. He was getting used to this nice cabin life and wished that he owned one. It seemed like a million miles away from the delta he grew up in, but he had started to enjoy the seclusion of the mountains with its rocks and trees and clear streams instead of the flat fields you could see for miles across, and its muddy ditches. It was almost like a new start. He wished that his mother hadn't died, that he married the girl of his dreams, and that he had moved here to these mountains. As he drifted off to sleep and his mind was in between that area of being awake or dreaming, it was here that his subconscious questioned whether he was really hearing the voice of God or not when he had killed everyone. He knew he was supposed to have been on medication but hadn't taken it in months. Was that why he had believed God had spoken to him? He wished that it was a new start, but sadly knew that it wasn't. He would either meet his fate a little later on in life, maybe weeks, months, or years, or it would be within the next few days.

Michael Delacroix was awake before dawn and had already had his morning breakfast of coffee and marshmallows, plus a few crackers. He tidied up and was out the door and into the surrounding woods, walking towards his next destination, the Victorian Cabin, before daylight. He wanted to scope the area around it out and hide before the couple made their rounds. He figured for sure they would, since they had missed it last night. Apparently due to him and the surprise he had made for them. It was about time to create another one today.

He made it to the next cabin in good time. All this walking had really improved his stamina and his feet felt so much better. He still needed some shoes that fit.

****

Frank and Shelly woke up naturally to the sun shining in through the window instead of an alarm. There was something so comforting and peaceful about waking up with morning sunlight shining right in your eyes, especially if you didn't have to go to work.

They were shocked to see that they had slept in past 8AM because the clock on the nightstand read 8:47AM. They felt well rested. All of a sudden they realized that they had forgotten to make their rounds to all of the cabins last night before they went to bed and decided they had better get a move on. They showered and dressed in jeans and t-shirts, unsure yet of what else they wanted to do for the day.

As they drove the familiar route, they talked about their options. They had enjoyed the town and all of its quaint attractions for the last three days and wondered what lay beyond the hills of Mountain View. They knew there were resort towns not far away and since they had pretty much been roughing it, they decided it might be fun to explore their surroundings and go see what they could see.

They checked all of the cabins and the office and noting that all seemed fine, they went back to their cabin and pulled up the two resort towns of Greers Ferry and Heber Springs on their laptop. Greers Ferry was the closest, so they decided to check it out first.

As they left out of town using their GPS toget them from town to country, they drove past big open fields surrounded by mountains. It was a beauty they rarely witnessed.

They took in all the twists and curves in the road and began noticing some of the little names of towns or spots in the road they passed through.

The name of the first town to catch their attention was Sunnyland on Hwy 9 just outside of Mountain View. Another name, they read on a road sign, that was not in the direction they were going, was Turkey Creek. They kept going until Hwy 9 turned into Hwy 263 past Parma, headed towards a town called Prim.

Prim, it turned out, was a very small community with a population of only 471 people. What it lacked in size, it made up for in beauty. There were a couple of gas stations/convenience stores, a restaurant, and three churches. After crossing a bridge over a creek, they went up yet another mountain the locals called "Bear Mountain Road", and came out on Hwy 92, that took them straight into Greers Ferry.

Greers Ferry was a tourist town mainly for its largest attraction, Greers Ferry Lake. There were several places to shop, including a clothing store, a video rental store, antique and souvenir shops. There was a roadside market for fresh fruits and vegetables and local honey and preserves, which was just getting geared up with the first wares of spring. Frank and Shelly stopped and bought a jar of fresh local honey.

It was almost noon, so they stopped in at a local

restaurant and ordered a sandwich to go and asked where there might be a pretty place to sit and eat. The owner of the place told them to go to the Narrows Park, just across the bridge, and watch the boats. It was very scenic and they enjoyed the view as they sat at a concrete table to eat their lunch. There were several boats up and down the lake. The lake itself was trimmed with large outcroppings of rock at one end and an island in the middle of the lake on the other end. Both ends were surrounded by mountains.

They had found a marina with boat rentals close by and decided to see the lake up close and personal. They had already taken a few photos of the Narrows Bridge from their table and knew if the lake was that pretty from the edge, it would be awesome right down on it. They rented a ski boat for two hours. Armed with sunglasses and cameras, they sliced down the middle of Greers Ferry Lake.

It was breathtaking. They were as pleased with the view, and maybe even more so, than they had been on the White River in Mountain View. This lake opened up to wide spectacular views all around. The water was a pretty blue green and houses dotted the mountains. They boated from one end to the other and around the little island named "Goat Island", named for the wild goats that inhabited it. Shelly got some photos of some of them as they idled near the shore.

They noticed that their time was almost up, and it was time to head back to the marina. The sky overhead was looking a little stormy as well, with large black clouds looming overhead. They were almost back to the dock when the rain broke loose and poured down on them as they sped under the Narrows Bridge. It was a cold rain and they couldn't wait to get out of it and back in Cecil's truck. As soon as they returned the boat and jumped in the truck, they turned the heater on full blast until they began to warm up. They were almost back to Mountain View by the time they felt comfortable again and their clothes had started to dry out.

****

Michael Delacroix had been rummaging through the Victorian Cabin with a vengeance and had found more goodies. He had found some cans of tuna this time and finally, someone had left some soft drinks and chips behind. He had already stuffed himself with the various combinations of food from there and what he carried in his sack, and had sat back to think of what he could do to create more work for the couple. It was then that he noticed the dead tree on the edge of the yard. It was still standing, but supported by another tree's branches. One good strong wind, and it would come down...right into the round sitting room that was surrounded with glass windows. One swift kick might do the trick. He walked over to the tree and pushed on it hard. It had bounce, but didn't fall. He pushed again as hard as he could, bouncing against it. Still no luck. Finally he climbed upon it and began jumping up and down. He could feel it starting to give way. Finally, with a cracking of branches, it began to break loose from the branches that held it in place. Michael Delacroix had to leap off as it fell hard into the roof of the house, breaking through the edge of the overhang, and into one of the large windows, shattering the glass. It was a mess.

This one would take them a while to fix. He would now sit in the woods and wait until they came to do their check before moving on to the next cabin. He was done here at this one. It would be a while yet before they came back. Anyway it usually was, so he thought he would walk back up to the office again to make sure it was still vacant.

Michael Delacroix had walked up onto the porch and looked in the windows. It was still like it was the last time he had checked. The door was also locked and the lights off. He walked around to the back and saw no evidence anyone had been there either. He was walking back around to the front and his mind was off in another world when he was startled.

"Hey man…" a male voice said. Michael Delacroix actually jumped as he looked toward the man from which the voice came.

He was a lanky looking guy, probably in his thirties, with short, wiry, red hair and a light beard. He wore a floppy green fishing hat, a t-shirt with holes and dirt on it, and cargo shorts with bulging pockets. He had on a pair of worn out tennis shoes.

"Hey, the guy started again, I've been hitchhiking all the way from Missouri and made it to here. I'm trying to get to Virginia and I need a little cash. If you're the owner, I was wondering if you might need a little help around here…you know, for extra cash. I can chop wood or run errands or fix things."

It was there in that instant that he got his first feelings that this guy wasn't here to work. God had sent him here for Michael Delacroix to rid the earth of him. He was a shifty individual who was careless in where he trod and that was his mistake. Michael Delacroix asked him the single most important question of: "If I told you that this was the worst day of my life and I felt like I was going to kill myself, would you help me? Do you believe in God and would you pray with me?"

"Whoa....I didn't say I could be a counselor or a preacher, I just want to work for money. I need somebody to help *me*!" The hitchhiker said shaking his head and waving his arms about from side to side with a semi-serious look on his face.

Michael Delacroix stood studying him for a moment and then asked the last question that the hitchhiker would ever answer. "What size shoes do you wear?"

"A size 12. Why?"

"Take them off." Michael said pointing at his feet.

The hitchhiker gave him a funny look, but bent over to take off a shoe. When he did, Michael brought his knee up and rammed it into the guy's nose, breaking it instantly. Blood was pouring out of it. The guy was screaming and his hands flew up to his face. Michael quickly grabbed a stick of wood from the porch and hit him over the head with it again and again until he wasn't moving.

He had to hide the body. He quickly grabbed the body under the arms and started dragging it away from the front of the office. Blood was everywhere on the ground. He dragged the body all the way into the woods, then stood there wiping sweat and the hitchhiker's blood out of his eyes. Finally he turned the body face down and weighted it down with as many rocks as he could find. As he got down to the legs, he pulled off the dead body's tennis shoes and switched them out with his boots. He slipped his feet inside the tennis shoes. They were still warm and he could feel the pattern that the other man's feet had molded into the padding inside of them. They were so comfortable it felt like he didn't even have any shoes on. He would be able to walk so much faster. He would definitely have to re-wash his clothes and take a shower tonight.

    As soon as he was satisfied with covering the body, he went back to the front of the office and scooped up handfuls of dirt from another spot a few feet away and covered the blood up as best as he could. It was still visible, but there wasn't anything else he could do to cover it. He wished it would rain and wash it away. Maybe the couple would think that an animal had been killed here and carried off. He didn't have long to worry about it because he could hear the roar of the truck as it came rumbling over the gravel. It was time to hide. He ran into the woods and hid until they passed. After they were out of sight he took off running back towards the Victorian Cabin to wait until they came to do their rounds before he moved on to the next cabin. He wanted to see the look on their faces as they saw the damage and what to do with it.

****

    Frank and Shelly, even though almost dried off, wanted to change into some clean clothes. They grabbed another pair of jeans and t - shirt, and quickly changed. It was past 4PM and they still had time to go out to eat and see what else they would like to do the next day. They decided to go check on all of the cabins first this time before they forgot again, or it got dark. Then they would have that job over with for the day and could relax.

They had checked all of the five cabins that were duplicates and then started back on the side that their cabin was on. They had gotten almost to the end and were feeling great when they saw it. The Victorian Cabin definitely had problems.

A tree had fallen and had broken a section of the roof off, and had smashed the glass window. They stood there wondering what to do. They decided it was another trip back to Hipp Modern Builders.

They jumped in the truck and hurried off before closing. When they got to the store, Gentry was walking out of his office from behind the front counter and smiled when he saw them.

"Decided to come back to see us cause you like us, or do you have another problem with the PVC pipes?" He asked smiling.

They explained what had happened and then told him they didn't have the first clue what to do with it since they couldn't replace the window themselves, but wanted to at least make it secure enough that animals or a person couldn't break in and do more damage. Frank had taken some photos of it on his cell phone and showed them to Gentry. It gave him a much better idea of just how bad it was and what it would take to patch the hole.

First, he said they would need a chain saw to cut the tree up to move it, and that Hipp Modern Builders had equipment that they could rent and bring back when they were through. He had a chainsaw that would do the trick. Then he also let them rent a hammer and he thought that a couple of sheets of plywood would patch the hole from the broken window, so they bought that and a box of nails and rented a power cord and a skill saw to cut it with. It didn't look like the roof had bad enough damage that it would need a tarp, so they decided to let Cecil take care of that when he returned. Gentry suggested they get some safety goggles too. He had some guys load the plywood on the truck for them and he followed them out to the truck. He joked with them about needing a vacation from their vacation and hoped that they were still enjoying themselves in between all the repairs they were having to make. He reminded them that if they needed anything else or didn't know how to do something, to give him a call.

They went back to the Victorian Cabin and unloaded their materials. They didn't have the slightest idea that they were being watched from the woods. As soon as Frank started up the chainsaw, Michael Delacroix slipped silently through the woods and back down the road to his next cabin, the Contemporary style. He wouldn't have to worry about them making rounds again tonight.

Michael Delacroix decided that this would be the last cabin he would "move to". His feet had healed up, and with the new shoes they wouldn't hurt at all. He had found enough food to satisfy him for a few days until he could get somewhere else, far away from here.

He had found even more food in this house. There were several cans of vegetable soup with meat in it, some fruit cocktail, also in cans, and a box of cereal and some cheese. This would be the best food yet. Tonight he feasted on soup with cheese and crackers, and washed it down with a Coke.

He had to try to think of a way to get a vehicle. He still didn't feel like he needed to kill the couple and if he did, he knew people would be looking for them and then for that truck. The hitchhiker he had killed wouldn't be missed for a long time. Probably nobody knew he had wound up there in the first place. If he stole their truck, he would have to have the keys. He knew they kept the keys with them at all times. He entertained the thought of breaking in at night when they were asleep to steal them, but he didn't want to make a mistake and get caught. If they saw him, then they could identify him and the police would be hot on his trail. That would be bad. He didn't want that to happen. He would have to think about this very hard. It kept swirling around and around in his mind.

It was after dark when he went to bed. He had thought until he fell into a hard, deep, fitful sleep. He dreamt all night of killing and of running. Tossing and turning, even in his sleep he could hear the sound of the dogs barking and the officers yelling as they trailed him through the woods again. Sweat pouring off of his body as he ran, and in real life on the pillow he slept on in the floor of the cabin.

****

It took a couple of hours to get the tree cut up and moved out of the way and then get the plywood over the broken windows. They were satisfied that they had done a good job and that the cabin was secure from animals or humans breaking in. They took the chainsaw and skill saw back to their own cabin and left them there while they went to eat.

The last place they needed to check on before they went to eat was the office. They hopped out of the truck and Frank went to the back while Shelly tried the front door. It was locked. Everything inside seemed fine. She turned to go back to the truck and could see Frank coming from around the side of the building. She had gotten halfway across the yard when she looked down and saw it. There was a large area of dark dirt that was different from all the other dirt around it. Frank saw that she had stopped and came over to see what she was looking at.

"Look." She pointed at the ground.

"It looks recent. Frank said as he bent down to inspect the ground closer. It looks like….blood." He picked up some of the dirt between his fingers and felt of it. A red cast showed up on his skin through the crumbles of dirt. He looked up at her with a startled expression.

"It *is* blood!" Shelly exclaimed. They both wondered how it got there and why there was so much of it. Where had it came from?

They got back in the truck and started for town. They thought as they went down the road. The only thing they could figure out, is that an animal of some type had killed another animal there and then drug it off to eat it. Maybe even a bear. But the puzzling thing was that it almost looked like it tried to cover up the blood. Did bears or animals do that? The whole yard was a thick type of grass, so there were no paw prints if it were an animal, and there had been no other people around for days besides them. As sure as they were that it was probably just animals, they still felt a little uneasy, but there was no cause to bring out the police because there was nothing to show them of a crime.

They finally got to the stoplight in town where they needed to take a turn that would take them to the restaurant they wanted to eat at tonight. They had decided on Mexican and there was a perfect looking place right next to the courthouse they had been wanting to try. They parked and Frank went on in to the restroom to wash his hands before they got seated. He didn't like that the dirt he had picked up had blood in it. In fact, it really bothered him, but he didn't want Shelly to know just how bad.

The Mexican food was just what they needed. The flavor was delicious and it was just the right degree of hotness and the atmosphere was outstanding with the rock floor and rock walls, the colored lights and colorful decorations. They feasted on chips and salsa and had chicken and beef burritos with rice and beans and large glasses of sweet tea. For dessert they had a plate of sopapillas with a sweet brandy butter sauce. When they finally got finished, it was getting dark outside. Even though they had been on the go all day and had been super busy, for once they weren't tired. They figured they had finally gotten accustomed to their vacation of fun and work. They decided to go to Walmart and buy a new

DVD to watch before going to bed.

They got one of the newest action movies out and a thriller movie, and grabbed a single bag of microwave popcorn with movie theatre butter. They went back to their cabin to enjoy their night. Cecil had left a stack of firewood on the front porch and they brought a few sticks in and placed them in the fireplace with some kindling, and made a cozy fire. Shelly got some heavy blankets from the closet upstairs and she and Frank curled up on the couch, in their sleeping attire, and munched on the popcorn while they watched their movie from the sixty inch flat screen TV on the wall.

Both movies were good and by the time they were over, it was after 11PM. Time to go to bed. So far, this had been a really fun vacation and they had enjoyed every minute of it. Even repairing the damaged cabins. They had decided that tomorrow, which was Thursday, they would get up early and take a drive to Heber Springs and see what they could see. They had enjoyed Greers Ferry and thought Heber Springs would be fun and relaxing. They had already been on their laptops and found some places where they wanted to go and saw some things they wanted to do.

They crawled in bed and turned out the lamp light on their nightstand. They tried to count the stars out their bedroom window, giggling as they counted.

"I don't know if you felt it, but I had the creepiest feeling while we were working on the Victorian Cabin. Like someone was watching us. Did you feel like that?" Shelly asked Frank.

"It's just your imagination, especially now that we

found that blood. Don't worry. Everything is ok. We're just out in the country and things happen." Frank assured her. Before they knew it, they were sound asleep.

Thursday

Chapter 9

Frank and Shelly had set their alarm clock this time so they would have plenty of time to go exploring. They got up at 7AM ready for a big day. With their cameras, they jumped in Cecil's truck and made their rounds for the morning. Everything was fine and they hoped it would be when they got back. The last two days in a row, they'd had to work on something.

They drove the same route they had the day before until they got to the junction of Hwy 263 and Hwy 92. They took a left instead of a right to go to Heber Springs. They enjoyed looking at the names of the towns again. One in particular stood out to them, a little town named Drasco. It reminded them of an old west town where gunfighters had shootouts. Another town that they liked the name of, was Tumbling Shoals. It sounded pretty, exactly like a river rippling over rocks, and they added it to their list they had made of neat places they had been to on their vacation.

When they made it to Heber Springs, the first thing they stopped at was the Greers Ferry Dam which, even though they were in Heber, the dam was where Greers Ferry Lake joined the Little Red River of Heber Springs. There was a lookout of sorts that President John F. Kennedy stood at, and dedicated the dam in 1963 just a few weeks before he was shot and killed. It was a beautiful area, with plaques and a bust of Kennedy that added a glimpse of the importance of that visit he had made. Frank and Shelly was glad they had happened upon it.

Less than a mile down the road they toured a fish hatchery that was very interesting. It produced fish that stocked the Little Red River and other streams in Arkansas.

After touring that, they turned around and went back the way they had come to a road that took them to Sugar Loaf Mountain. It basically was a mountain with a rim of rock all the way around its crown at the top. It was a common place to hike and you could see for miles all the way around it while standing on the top. It was beautiful from the ground and though Frank and Shelly weren't prepared for a hike that big, and they made a promise that they would come back and hike it before they returned home. It had a neat history behind it of the early Indian and white settlers and had served as a landmark to them on their travels.

After taking photos of Sugar Loaf from the ground, they went to Bridal Veil Falls. It wasn't too much of a hike and they were so glad they had gone. It was a beautiful waterfall that was wide and long with a backdrop of rock behind it and water that cascaded down into a beautiful stream below over large moss covered rocks. They couldn't wait to get their photos uploaded to their laptops to e-mail to their friends and family.

After that they decided to shop on the main street where the original town of Heber Springs started. It also had old buildings similar to the ones in Mountain View. Many of them now housed local crafts and antiques. They were also directly across and down the street from the Heber Springs court house. Where Mountain View was quaint and seemed more secluded, Heber Springs was more of a tourist town with many more modern stores and businesses. They enjoyed the slight difference and had a good time shopping.

They enjoyed a walk in Spring Park after shopping and got a taste of water from seven different springs in Spring Park that provide waters known as White Sulphur, Red Sulphur, Black Sulphur, Arsenic, Iron, Magnesia, and Eye Water, that supposedly had "healing properties". Frank and Shelly mostly thought they just smelled bad. The Sulphur in the water had a smell much like rotten eggs.

After going to a few more stores, they decided that it was time to go back to Mountain View. It was almost 5PM and they would need to make their rounds and eat supper somewhere. The drive back was fun as they recounted their day and all they had seen. They had taken so many photos. They couldn't be happier if they had gone to a tropical island.

The route back to the cabin was easy, since they had already gone that way before and they remembered certain places they had passed. This time they got a chance to really look at some farms and houses. The land here in this state was really pretty and there were some gorgeous homes with neatly manicured lawns and beautifully landscaped yards. One thing they kept seeing were these "round rocks". They finally got so curious that when they stopped to get gas in Prim, they both got out and asked about them when they went in the store. The owner told them that the round rocks were caused from a unique combination of chemical formation, compression, and erosion over 300 million years ago that caused them to become round, and that they had been used in Prim as decorations on lawns for years.

Frank and Shelly thanked her. She told them to take a left out of the store parking lot and go to the church on the top of the hill. There they could find some large rocks to take photos of. The church had used then to decorate the church yard and the parking lot. She also told them to stop at the post office in Prim and take photos of the ones there that lined the driveway.

They paid for their gas and drove where she had told them to. There were round rocks of all sizes, varying in their shape and color. One, in someone's yard they had passed looked almost like a peanut, and others were shaped like giant snowballs. They took photos of them from different angles and with each of them, Frank or Shelly, sitting on some of the larger ones. What a strange phenomenon, but so very interesting and pretty.

When they were done, they kept going straight past the gray brick post office, back towards Stone County and Mountain View.

****

Michael Delacroix had been busy all day. Busy thinking. He needed a vehicle. The only thought that kept popping into his head was taking the truck that the young couple was driving. He had finally decided that he was going to have to sneak in while they were asleep, get the keys, and be long gone in the truck before they woke up and noticed it was gone. That way, he would have a big jump before the police started looking for it or knew it was associated with him. Tonight wouldn't be a good night to do it though. If he were to steal it on the weeknight or weekday, there would be more traffic from rush hour in the cities and he might get noticed easier. People slept later on Saturday and the going would be more smooth. Besides, he dreaded it. He had actually enjoyed himself here, as much as any man on the run could, and dreaded to run again. The nightmares he'd had last night left him almost exhausted when he woke up that morning. Having to worry about food and shelter was another worry, but he knew his time was running out here and he may have already stayed too long. His plans were to try to steal the keys on Friday night and be on the road in minutes afterwards. Tonight he would enjoy another meal of soup and all the trimmings and try catch up on some more sleep. Hopefully without nightmares. Friday night would come soon enough.

     Frank and Shelly made it back to Mountain View and it was almost dark when they returned to the cabins to make their rounds. They started with the cabins on the far side of the property and then ended up at the office and on around until they got to their own. Happily, nothing was damaged and everything was locked up tight. They were glad because they were tired. So tired that they didn't notice that at the Contemporary Cabin there was a faint smell of soup cooking that made its way out through the miniscule cracks, crevices and vents that every house had, and into the evening air. They were so full and had gotten so comfortable in their routine of everything being secure, that they didn't notice…and even Michael Delacroix had gotten lax in his hiding and being alert, that he actually missed the sound of the truck crunching across the driveway. In fact, he didn't notice it until Frank had walked upon the front porch and jiggled the doorknob. Michael Delacroix quickly dove down on the floor, crawling away from the back kitchen door and around a corner before Shelly could get there to check that lock. His heart was racing as he mentally chewed himself out for being so careless. They finally left and he returned to his soup, shutting off the burner just as it was boiling over.

Frank and Shelly finally got back to their own cabin and went inside to load all of their photos onto their laptops and into an online website for safe-keeping in case their computer were to quit working or they lost their micro SD card. They had taken so many, it took a while. They enjoyed looking at them as they relaxed by the fire, after they were finally loaded. So far they had taken over 500 photos since they left New York.

They sent some e-mails out to their friends and family that they were having a blast and were doing ok and couldn't wait to see everyone when they got back to the city. Around 9PM, they took their showers and got into bed to read some of their book. They drifted off to sleep before midnight with their book still in the bed with them.

Court Square

Chapter 10

They didn't wake up until 9AM Friday morning. It actually felt so good they just lay there for a while and talked until Shelly's stomach started growling. Frank knew that when that happened it wouldn't be long before she got grouchy and irritable if she didn't get something to eat. They both got up and dressed in jeans and t-shirts. They did all the cabin checks and headed off to town for breakfast in record time.

They had already decided what they wanted to do for the day. They hadn't really been shopping at all of the little shops in Mountain View, so they decided to see what they could find. Then they planned to wind up on the Court Square for music that evening.

They started with some antique shops that lined the road on the way into town. They saw all manners of farm implements and tools that they would never have known what they were, except for the tag on them with their name and dishes from days long past. After those places, they went on closer to town and stopped at a couple of novelty shops and craft stores, finding country quilts, doilies, and knick-knacks of all kinds.

They got down on Main Street and there were so many little shops of antiques and handmade crafts, which they took their time and went to every one they came to. There were handmade clothes in one store. Wood carved furniture from cedar, oak, and pine in another with accessories of animal pelts and hides to decorate a country home. There were handmade iron works on one side of the street and pottery on another. One store had leather goods from purses to horse saddles. There were more antique stores and stores with custom printed t-shirts and totes. People bustled here and there, up and down the little country sidewalks, much like they did the streets of New York, but on a much smaller scale and in much less of a hurry.

It was around 2PM that they finally made their way down to where the truck was parked. They bought a t-shirt there and had bought several things along the way. Everything was getting so hard to carry they decided to leave them in the truck. It felt good to get rid of their load.

They got their packages unloaded and locked up and walked over to a rock wall that went around the courthouse square and took a seat on the wall to wait for the musicians, who were already setting up their equipment, to start playing.

Before long, a crowd of people had gathered on the square. Some brought lawn chairs to sit in and some brought blankets to spread out on the ground. Frank and Shelly could tell that this was a normal thing here that many of the people who lived here attended often. It was casual and friendly with a lot of chattering amongst everyone.

Neither one of them knew anything about Bluegrass, but they were about to find out. The first band that stepped up to play were three young boys in their teens that played a guitar and a mandolin. They called themselves The Six Ridge Boys. They sang some Bluegrass favorites. Their voices harmonized together beautifully and they could play their instruments, skillfully, as well as anyone Frank and Shelly had ever seen at any other concert before. It took talent to play as well as they did. Frank and Shelly were amazed. They did one more song that was a slow ballad with a haunting melody. It was about a young man who had gone into the military during the civil war and left his wife and unborn child at home. He would write her of the battles he had been in and of the killing he had seen on both sides and how he couldn't wait to be with her once again, but before he made it home he got killed in the last battle. The lyrics and music were both sad and beautiful at the same time. The three young teens sang it with all the tone of experience that any professional grown men would sing it. Frank and Shelly sat holding hands, enraptured at the story that unfolded in the words as they sang.

After they were through, an older group of men called The Timbo Tenors, sang with a banjo and a fiddle. They were good also, but in a fun light hearted way. Their song was about coon hunting and was funny. They had the audience laughing.

The next group that got up had a male and female duo that sang a Bluegrass gospel song. Frank and Shelly had never heard it before and simply thought it was the most touching song they had ever heard. The music and words stirred a deep sense of emotion within both of them. At one point, they even stopped the music and sang the rest of it with no instruments at all, a style called a Capella. Frank and Shelly had to wipe tears by the time it was over. A man and his wife, that were sitting close to them told them that that bluegrass group was local and sang at their church every Sunday morning and invited them to come and hear them sing and attend a service while they were on vacation. Frank and Shelly thanked them and told them they might do that.

There was an intermission during some of the entertainment, so Frank and Shelly decided to run to the only restroom available to the whole square. It was about fifty yards from where they sat and they heard conversations among people as they walked. One in particular caught their attention.

"Yeah, he escaped from the prison at Calico Rock and out ran the officers and dogs and they think he might've came this way. Somebody reported their canoe stolen the day after he escaped."

Frank and Shelly stopped to listen in. They found out that the escaped felon was going to prison for several murders in Louisiana and Arkansas and was dangerous. They didn't know how exactly that he had escaped, but they hadn't found him yet and the Mountain View police department was actively searching and keeping a lookout for him.

They thanked the locals for sharing the information with them because since they had been on vacation they had not turned on the TV or radio since they got there and hadn't bought a newspaper or even had any clue of what had been going on. The locals were more than happy to tell them, since nothing that exciting had happened around there like that that they could ever remember. Frank and Shelly continued on toward the restroom talking as they went. As awful as it was, it just seemed to make their vacation all the more interesting.

That was until they remembered the blood they had found in front of the office. Still seeming far-fetched that the one person that had escaped would end up at their cabin site and leave a pool of blood, Frank and Shelly shrugged it off. After all, she and Frank were still alive and they had been the only ones on the property since Cecil and his family had left days ago. There was no one to kill but them. They decided to keep their eyes open though, now that they knew a killer was loose.

They stayed at the Court Square until all of the entertainment was over and headed back to their cabin. They had enjoyed their whole day and all of the stuff they had bought. They got a cup of coffee at a fast food drive through to drink with some homemade pies they had bought shopping that day. They decided to eat them while they watched the local television station to catch the news that night and see if they could see any more about the escaped felon. This would be another interesting thing to tell their friends and family about when they got home.

The couple had been gone all day and it was way after dark and they were still not back yet. Not that this really made a difference. Michael Delacroix had planned all day and had finally gotten everything as ready as he could. He had hidden his sack of food near the entrance of the cabin resort, just off the highway, before the office was even in view. He had planned on jumping out to get it after he stole the truck, in hopes it would help sustain him until he could get far enough away to get more.

He had decided he would sit in the edge of the woods and watch and wait until their lights went out in the cabin, and even wait for an hour or two after that, to pick the lock and sneak in. He hoped that like anybody else, they would just throw the keys down somewhere on the bottom floor and not take them upstairs with them. It would be so easy if they would just do that. If they hadn't, then he would almost surely have to kill them. The chances of them not waking up while he was climbing the stairs and then fumbling around in the dark to find the keys, was very remote. He didn't have a flashlight and wasn't going to use matches or the grill lighter. The strike of the match was almost as loud as the click of the lighter and would just make him all the more nervous.

He had just then left his sack of food in its hiding place, and was walking back towards the couple's cabin when he heard the crunching of tires turning in from the highway, onto the gravel road. He jumped back into the woods. It was them. He saw the truck slow and pull to a stop in front of the office as the man got out and went up to the door. He saw the female get out and walk a few feet in front of the truck and stop, looking down. Then he heard her scream. He shifted his position and tried to get a better look. What had she seen? A snake? She just stood there frozen, her male companion rushing toward her. He could see them talking animated with their actions, a look of bewilderment on their faces. Now she had her hands over her eyes to block out whatever it was she had been looking at. It must not have been a snake. Then it hit him. The body.

Horrified, Shelly covered her eyes in disbelief at the sight before her. It was the severed hand of a man. She and Frank could tell that it had been chewed on by animals and appeared to not have been gone from the rest of the body for very long, because it looked like it could almost reanimate, make a fist, and wiggle its fingers. Shelly realized then that she had seen way too many horror movies over the years, and quickly pushed the thought out of her mind. As they both talked hurriedly about what they should do next, they realized that they themselves might be in danger where they stood. From either the animal that had left the hand or the animal that might have killed the body it had been attached to. After what they heard at the Court Square, the possibility of a murderer now seemed like reality and not just a story. They knew they had to report this to the police department. Frank took out his cell phone and tried to make a call. Cecil, true to his word, had told them that the cell phone service was not good here. It wasn't a lie. Frank had no signal at all. Shelly tried also and it was the same. They knew that leaving the hand where it was, was not an option. Some other animal might carry it off before they could get back to it and then they would look crazy. One of them could stay with it while the other took the truck either back to the cabin and called law enforcement or out on the road far enough to get cell service, but they didn't want to leave each other alone. After talking it over, they finally decided the best thing was to let Frank stay with the hand while Shelly took the truck back to their cabin to call the police. They decided to take photos of it with their cells to show exactly where it was when they found it in relation to the office. They used both of their cells to photography it from different angles, and placed an ink pen next to it for size reference. They wanted to have proof in case someone or something came back to get it and killed Frank before Shelly could get back to him in the truck.

Frank gave her the card out of his wallet with the number to the police department Cecil had written down for them and she slipped it into her back pocket, grabbed the keys from Frank and jumped into the truck. She fired up the motor and left a trail of dust illuminated by the taillights as she raced back toward the cabin. In just the short time it took her to drive down the crooked, tree lined road, she spooked herself at the thought of someone waiting for her in the dark on the cabin porch and almost turned back around to go back to Frank. She knew the call had to be made one way or the other. When she pulled up in front of the cabin, she left the headlights shining and quickly scanning with her eyes to see that no one was visible anywhere near the porch, she ran for the cabin door with the keys in her hand. She had the door unlocked in less than five seconds and once she was inside, she switched on the lights and relocked it. Grabbing the number out of her back pocket, she ran towards the phone and quickly punched the buttons.

"Mountain View Police Department." She heard the voice of a man answer.

"Yes, sir...I'm not sure how to say this, but we are on vacation and we've just found a severed hand that we would like to show you. No sir, this is not a joke." Shelly explained where they were and where they had seen the hand. She told them that Frank stayed behind with it while she ran back to call the police. The dispatcher told her that someone would be there in a few minutes and asked her if they would please remain where they were and reminded her not to touch the hand until they arrived. As soon as she hung up the phone, she went back out the door, locking it as she left, and got back in the truck to go back to Frank. She just hoped he was still there and alright. As she rounded the last little curve in the gravel road, she could see him standing there waiting for her. She told him what the dispatcher had said and they stood there close to each other as they waited for someone to get there. It wasn't long before not one officer, but five cruisers arrived with a total of nine officers.

As official as they were, the looks on their faces was priceless. As the local person in town had told them, this was not an everyday occurrence in Mountain View, and the officers seemed almost as excited as Frank and Shelly.

They also took photos of the hand and then placed it into a paper bag, where it would eventually be given a case number, then sealed and placed in a freezer to preserve it as evidence. First, they would fingerprint it and see if they could find out who it had belonged to.

It would be easy to get prints off of it since it was in such good condition. Then they could run the prints through AFIS or Automated Fingerprint Identification System, which is a national fingerprint and criminal history system used by law enforcement at all hours of the day or night to solve and help prevent crime, and to catch criminals and terrorists. It is a very helpful system in that it not only matches fingerprints, but can also pull up the criminal history of someone who has broken the law. When someone goes to jail and gets fingerprinted, their prints are shared by each state, local, and federal law enforcement agencies. It can give their photo and tell important characteristics of that person such as what they look like and if they have any scars or tattoos. It will also tell if they go by any other names or aliases. The system doesn't only have criminals in it, but also has fingerprints of people have been or are still in the military or who may be government employees.

Everyone wondered if it could really be the serial killer. They supposed that it was possible. The threw around the idea it could've happened that someone had been in a freak accident of some sort and had gotten it chopped off by a mower or farm machine, and in their haste to get medical attention, had left the hand behind and a dog had carried it to where Frank and Shelly found it. The police department made a plan to check local hospitals to see if anyone had come in with those types of injuries.

****

As soon as the couple had picked up what looked like a hand from where Michael Delacroix was sitting, and he saw the female tear out of the office parking lot, he jumped up from his hiding place and ran toward the woods where he had buried the body. Sure enough, something had dug up enough of it to get an arm out and had chewed the hand off. The rest of the body was still there. What in the world was he going to do? He had to do something fast, if he didn't they would surely know something wasn't right. He had to move the body. It couldn't stay buried here in the makeshift grave he had made for it. He quickly threw the rocks off of it, throwing them far and wide. He gagged at the smell as he reached down and pulled the body up out of the ground by its clothing. It had started to decompose badly and he couldn't risk dragging it along the ground because of the trail it would leave. He hoisted it up over his shoulder and immediately threw up. As soon as he regained composure, he took off at a dead run towards the highway.

His thoughts were of throwing the body down hard on the road, then dragging it into a ditch and positioning it like it had been hit by a vehicle and then left to die. He knew they had ways of finding out for sure if that was really how the person had been killed. He didn't know exactly how long it would take them to figure it out, but it was at least a way to keep them guessing for a little longer. They wouldn't be able to know tonight.

He made it to the highway and jogged at least 100 feet or so past the entrance to the cabin resort. He found a place in the ditch that was pretty deep. Deep enough, he hoped, to not see a body that had been hit by a vehicle if you were driving down the road. He also knew the injuries to the body were not the right kind of injuries of getting hit by a vehicle. He took his foot and kicked the body in the ribs hard, several times, breaking and bruising it in an area where a truck should hit. He turned the body face down and twisted its legs around in crazy angles with the arms thrown wildly to the side. When he thought he had positioned it as good as he could, he took off running back into the woods.

He already knew that he couldn't make it back to the cabins for a while because they would be swarming with law enforcement. He just hoped they didn't have dogs that would be able to track him in any way. All he needed to do was get his sack of stuff he had left hidden at the entrance and get somewhere and stay out of sight for a while, but close enough to see what was going on. He would have to get back into one of the cabins as soon as they left because he had to wash his clothes and shoes and take a shower. The smell was unbearable. He didn't know if he would ever be able to eat again. He sure wished that people were not such bad people. If they had only believed in God and cared enough for each other to have prayed with him like they were supposed to, then he wouldn't have had to kill them.

He grabbed his sack of goodies that he had hidden and went back out to the highway, crossed it, and entered the woods on the other side. He got back behind the trees and into the darkness so that they couldn't see him, but he could see when they entered and when they left.

They all started pouring in. First it was the couple in their truck, followed by five patrol cars. He didn't see "K9 Unit" on any of them, so he assumed it was safe to say that there wasn't a dog. That was a relief. They might be able to find the body and might happen to stumble upon where it was buried while they were searching, but he hoped not. If they did find the first place it had been, then he might have problems.

He started worrying that maybe he shouldn't have moved the body from the first place at all. If where they found the hand was in the area where all of the blood was from when he had first killed the hitchhiker, then they would know that this might have been where he was killed instead of on the highway. What a coincidence that whatever animal chewed his hand off, had left it so close to the spot that he had been killed as if to say; "hey, this is where it happened". If he had left the body in the woods, and uncovered, then it would've looked like he had been dragged into the woods by animals, but then again, it could look like a person had drug him into the woods. It was hard to know how it would look or what they would think. Either way, it was too late to worry now.

It would be a long night and he settled in to wait. He knew at some point they should be searching out by the roadway and he might have to get ready to move if they even looked like they were coming his way. He had gotten far enough back in the woods that they wouldn't be able to hear him if he quietly slipped away. He tried not to leave any evidence of anyone sitting there watching, so he remained as still as he could, not rustling up the leaves and trying not to break branches around him. He hoped the police officers didn't have noses like dogs. He smelled so bad it seemed that anyone could track him from a mile away. The night air was slightly cool, which helped, and it was still. From his hiding place he could hear the night sounds of frogs hollering that spring was here. That sound used to be a pleasant, comforting sound, but tonight it was a sound that helped cover up any noise he might make if he had to start walking. He leaned back against a large rock to wait. That was all he could do.

Frank and Shelly pulled up into the office parking lot again a few feet away from where they had found the hand. Behind them, the patrol units parked in zig zags, with their blue strobe lights flashing in such rapid sequence that each move anyone made was like being out on a dance floor at a wild party. Finally, all but one unit shut their lights off and just left on the high beams which helped cut out the visual distortion. The officers all followed Frank and Shelly over to the spot with their flashlights ablaze to see where they had found the hand.

One of the officers questioned them about being on vacation and Frank showed them the card that Cecil had given them and explained the circumstances of their being there while Cecil and his family were gone. They told them that he had asked them to check on each cabin every morning and every night to make sure there were not any other people staying in them without permission, and to make sure they were all locked and nothing gone wrong on the property. They went into detail about having had to fix various things that had gone wrong during the week and having to buy materials at Hipp Modern Builders, but that each cabin was always locked and nothing seemed amiss at any time. They had felt perfectly safe during their stay until they had heard the conversation at the Court Square about the serial killer and then found the hand.

The officers were very intent and serious when listening to their recount of their week. They had seemed impressed at how they had made their rounds and had explained that each cabin had been locked every day and night that they had checked. When they found out that Frank was a lawyer and what kind of criminals he put away, it seemed to help ease the officer's tension about who they were. Just as a precaution, they asked for Cecil's cell phone number to verify that he had indeed entrusted them with the care of his cabins and had given them permission to stay there rent free while he was away. They promised that they would not alarm him or tell him about the hand, but only that they were still searching for a dangerous person and just needed to be sure of who everyone was. They didn't see a need to make him come home from his vacation early from being scared that things weren't being taken care of, as they could tell that Frank and Shelly had done their best to watch over the place.

One of the officers stepped away and got back into his patrol unit to call Cecil while the others scrutinized the patch of ground where Frank and Shelly had found the hand. They bent over and looked closer at the ground for any clues. Remembering how the ground had looked bloody a few days before, Frank showed that area to them and told them about how he had picked some dirt up in his fingers and saw blood on his hands. He told them that they had debated on saying anything about it to the police because there was no body or no crime that they could see had been committed, and thought that some animal might have been killed there. They didn't want the police to think they were stupid, so they just pushed it to the side and didn't worry about it anymore.

There was nothing to be seen on the ground now, since it was dark and it had been a few days since they had found it like that. One of the officers went to his car and brought back some evidence collection pouches and a small garden spade and took samples of dirt from several different places. He said that first they would test it for blood, and then once they found which sample had blood in it, they would send it to the Arkansas State Crime Lab to determine if the blood was animal or human. The only drawback was that it might take a day or two to get the results. This might, however, help them to determine whether a crime had been committed there or not.

The rest of the officers had fanned out about five feet

between each other to see if they could find more evidence or a body. It was dark and hard to see even with their Maglite and Stinger flashlights. They had called in some auxiliary officers to help with the search so they could cover more area. Some of them had just arrived as well as the Sergeant over that shift. He directed them to search the perimeter of the property into the wood line while the officers in uniform searched the main grounds and around the office. They were instructed to let them know if they found anything at all suspicious or that didn't go with the surroundings. The officer who had called Cecil had come back and reported that he had gotten in touch with him and had confirmed Frank and Shelly's stay there was as they had said, and they had assured him everything was fine and he didn't need to come home. Frank and Shelly were allowed to sit in Cecil's truck and watch the search as they were curious to see if they found anything.

    The search of the office yard and parking lot, as well as around the building itself, turned up nothing. The uniformed officers were moving out towards the wood line and the road in from the highway, when one of the auxiliary officers called out.

    "I might've found something!"

    Everyone rushed to where he was. He was just inside the wood line and pointed on the ground.

    "It looks like vomit." The Sergeant stated, with a disgusted look on his face. As gross as it was, he took a photo of it.

    "I'm not real educated in the study of vomit, the

auxiliary officer said smiling, and I know that there are some animals that do vomit, but this to me looks like human vomit. It's not in a nice little pile like animals usually leave, at least our cat does, and it seems to have been ejected from way up high by the way it's splattered and in a stream. Animals don't do that I don't think."

"I think I'd have to agree with you on that one. Good work. I'll go ask our vacationers if it was either one of them out here in the woods sick for any reason and rule them out."

The Sergeant walked off as they continued their search. Oblivious to them all, they had stepped right over the place where the body had been buried with the rocks piled on top of it. The rocks had been scattered in such a manner that it was not obvious, by anyone who had not known, that they had been used for that purpose. They looked like they had been lying where they were when God had formed them and placed them there centuries ago.

The Sergeant told Frank and Shelly what they had found and questioned them if either one of them had been sick or had vomited there and forgotten about it. They both shook their heads no and told him that they had been just fine. It appeared to be quite fresh, so there was no reason to call and ask Cecil the same question. He asked them if they had any visitors while they were there and again the answer was no. There had not even been a mail carrier as Cecil had told them he had the post office to hold all of his mail until he came home. The Sergeant thanked them and was about to walk off when a voice came over his radio.

Sergeant, we have a 10-69....repeat a 10-69 out here on

"the highway."

Frank and Shelly looked at him with questions in their eyes, clueless to the ten code over the radio. He looked up at them as his hand went to his lapel mic to answer "10-4" and he said; "They've found a body".

The Sergeant turned and walked away with a determined step, since now, things had gotten serious. Frank and Shelly just stared at each other with their mouths open, unable to say anything for a few seconds. When they finally found the words to talk Shelly was the first one to speak.

"Do you think it's the serial killer?"

"I don't know. Frank answered. We'll have to see what they found. I mean, they should be able to tell if they body was murdered. It shouldn't be long until they let us know something.

They sat there talking and imagining as they wondered what the officers were seeing. As much as they would have liked to see what they found, they knew that they would have to stay put. Frank had seen dead bodies before and certainly seen photos of them in his line of work, but Shelly had never seen one except at a funeral, and she had been to only a couple of those. The thought of seeing one freaked her out, but she had a curious streak too, Frank knew. Just seeing the hand would be enough to give her nightmares for years though, and it was best that she not experience the dead body.

When the Sergeant got close to the rest of the officers, they directed him back down the gravel road and out onto the highway. The auxiliary officers who had been searching the wood line had come to the edge of it next to the road. They were standing way above the ditch and could see down into it and had spotted the body. The Sergeant walked up to it, careful not to disturb any evidence that might be around it. He took photos of it from every angle as he was walking up. As of yet, he couldn't say that it was a murder or a hit and run simply since it was found near the highway. He could see that it was a male but was unable to see how old he was since his face was turned toward the ground. Both arms and legs were bent at odd angles but the main thing he did notice was that one hand was missing.

"I think we found out who the "hand" belongs to". He said aloud as he took a close up photo of that.

Decomposition had obviously set in, but the body hadn't been there for more than two or three days. He checked in the pockets for identification and didn't find anything. It wasn't completely uncommon these days for people not to have I.D. on them.

"Let's go ahead and call the coroner. It'll take him a while to get out here and we should be finished by the time he gets here." He instructed one of the other officers as he kept taking photos of the area.

While the officer stepped off to the side to call the coroner, the Sergeant and other officers walked upon the road.

"What do you think Sarg? One of the officers asked. Do you think this is a hit and run?"

He walked several yards further down shining his light back and forth across the highway. "I don't see any black marks from someone slamming on their brakes. He answered, still walking. It could have still been an accident. Maybe they didn't see him. Or it could've been deliberate. They could've ran him over on purpose. Or, he paused…the body could've been dumped there and not been a hit and run at all."

He had stopped walking and turned around to look at the officers. He stood there thinking for a minute before he said; "The body will tell us what we need to know."

With that he started taking photos of the lack of evidence that might just turn out to be evidence in its own way. Just because there isn't something visible, doesn't always mean that nothing happened there.

The coroner finally arrived and pronounced the body dead by saying; "Well, this un's sure 'nuf dead!" They rolled him over instantly noticing the lack of lividity, or the pooling of blood that looks like bruising, to the skin in the area that is closest to the ground and knew that he had not died in that position and had most likely been dumped there. The face, if the body had truly been left face down in the ditch, should've had a deep purple hue to it with the rest of the skin a pasty white on the back of his neck, but instead, the face was white and the back of his neck purple. His head had been beaten severely with a blunt object, and in fact, was quite possibly the immediate cause of death.

It was too late in the game to check for rigor mortis, as that had long come and gone. Temperature was no longer a factor now either, except to lend to the speed of decomposition. The warmer the temperature, the faster decomposition occurs. They had to be careful when rolling over or picking up the body. As decomposition progresses, tissues lose their integrity and skin will just start peeling or sloughing off. This was happening now. As they rolled the body over to turn it so they could slide a tarp under it, part of the skin over the shoulder blades just came off in their hands. More than one officer gagged and turned away.

They made sure to check the front pockets for I.D. and again found nothing. Not even money or change. All they found was gooey sludge that the skin, starting to decompose, allowed the fluids from the body which was starting to liquefy, to ooze into the pockets. They zipped him up in the yellow body bag and watched as the coroner and his deputy lifted the body onto a gurney and rolled it to the back of their van and then lifted it inside, slamming the doors shut afterward. Everyone did the necessary thank you's and the coroner got in the van headed to the State Crime Lab in Little Rock. As everyone was leaving to either go back to the cabin office to get in their vehicles, or to go back to work or home, the Sergeant and another officer stopped by Cecil's truck where Frank and Shelly sat, still waiting to hear what they had found. The Sergeant told them as much as he could, but Frank and Shelly had questions.

They asked the Sergeant if he knew who the man was or if he was local to which he replied that he did not know the man but had taken a quick set of finger prints to run in the system to see if they could get an I.D. and he also told them that the body was missing a hand. If the prints matched, then another officer would transport the hand to Little Rock where the body was. The next question concerned their own safety.

"Do you think it was the serial killer that everyone was talking about?" Frank asked?

The Sergeant took a deep breath and answered as truthfully as he could. "There's no way of confirming that right now. We rarely have murders in our town or county or even anywhere within probably a fifty mile radius or more, so I guess the odds go up that it could be, but I can't say 100% that it is."

"Should we be afraid to go back to the cabins?" Shelly wanted to know with a great look of concern on her face.

"Well, I don't want to jump to conclusions and tell you that you'd be safer somewhere else. It seems like a very safe place and you haven't seen anyone hanging around and all of the cabins have been locked. I assume there is a phone in your cabin?"

"Yes. They both answered. Our cell phones don't get a signal here or inside the cabin, but there is a phone in it."

"If it would make you feel more comfortable, I'll send one of our officers out a few times during the night until the morning shift to patrol this area, maybe even drive through the whole cabin resort to check on you during the rest of your stay." He offered.

"That would be great. We would really appreciate it. Frank said. We're pretty city savvy, but we have no real protection here with us and it would make us feel a lot better."

With that, they both shook his hand and he told them if

they saw anything else or had any questions not to hesitate to call the police department, and he would be letting them know if they found out anything else that would be of concern to them during their stay. He and the other officer got back into their patrol cars and drove away. Frank and Shelly were still sitting in the truck and all of a sudden they felt very alone and a little scared.

Besides feeling alone and scared, they also felt very hungry. It had been around 5PM when they had supper and around 9PM or so when they had the coffee and fried pies. Since then they had been scared and excited and it was now almost 4AM. They knew there were no restaurants open here past 10PM, and even the Wal-Mart closed at midnight. They really didn't want to go back to the cabin right then, so they decided to drive out and "Google" their choices to see how far away they would have to drive to find an open restaurant. It turned out that the closest I-Hop was over an hour away in Conway, but they decided to go anyway. The drive might settle their nerves and by the time they ate and got back to the cabins they would be exhausted enough to sleep.

Shelly put Conway, Arkansas in her GPS and they headed in that direction. It was a fairly straight drive going south toward Little Rock, the capital of Arkansas. Since it was still dark, there wasn't much to see and so they talked about the night's events. By the time they had gotten to Conway, they had come up with every scenario possible as to why the hand had been in the office yard and why the body had been found in the ditch. They had scenarios with the hand belonging to the body and scenarios with it not belonging to it. They also had made up stories of how the body had gotten killed, one story was it had met its fate by the serial killer they had heard about and another was by accident, and still another story was by locals getting revenge on the handless body for something. It was a little fun, and helped to get the seriousness off their minds.

They drove into the town of Conway, a much more populated town than Mountain View, Greers Ferry or Heber Springs put together, with lots of businesses and town all around. They passed the exit and on ramp that went straight to the freeway and after going through a couple more stoplights, pulled into the I-Hop parking lot. It was almost 5AM when they sat down to order.

Not the least bit ashamed for blowing their healthy eating habits after a night like they had, they both had coffee and milk. Frank had steak and eggs with a side order of toast and hash browns. Shelly had two fried eggs, bacon, hash browns and a side order of toast. It was delicious. It felt good to be amongst a fairly large amount of people this early in the morning and their mood lightened while they ate.

When they were finished it was daylight. They could see all of the businesses around them and decided to just take a tour of the city and drive around. They were impressed at what businesses the town had for its size and the cleanliness of it and its design. They wished they had more time to explore it and even go further on to Little Rock, but they were starting to feel the effects of all they had gone through the day before and the whole night. They headed back for Mountain View. Before they got halfway back they discussed how the whole night seemed surreal, like it had never happened and their fears of returning to their cabin erased by the sunlight and good food. Frank had started getting sleepy driving, so Shelly took over when they got to the "Bear Mountain" coming into Woodrow and Prim. In less than an hour, they had made it back to their cabin and had crawled into bed exhausted.

Saturday

Chapter 11

Someone else had also sat up until the crack of dawn and was also exhausted. Michael Delacroix had spent the night out in the woods. He had stayed awake to see the last of the police cars drive away and then see the couple in their truck leave too. He wondered where on earth they could be going that time of the night and so he had sat up to see when or if they came back. He desperately needed to get back into one of the cabins to take a shower and wash those clothes, and he needed some sleep. Since the police had come and gone it might be safe enough for that, but then he had to get gone. He wanted to make sure he knew if the couple came back so he would know whether or not to expect them to be checking doors again.

It had been daylight now for about two hours and he had been nodding off to sleep. He hoped he wouldn't miss them driving in so he stood up and walked around to wake up. Just as he did, he saw their truck pull in the gravel road and head back off into the woods. He made a dash to the edge of the woods to make sure nobody else was coming and then ran across the road and into the woods on the other side. He went at an angle, so as to head them off faster and make it to the woods by the office first. He got there seconds before they did and watched them stop their truck and get out just like always.

Assuming that they would do that at every one, he took his time walking back to the next cabin, since he couldn't beat them to it. He would walk to it and then pick the lock and wait a few minutes before going to sleep to make sure no one else was going to show up and then he was going to crash.

When he made it there and got inside, he took his clothes off and immediately threw them into the washing machine and jumped into the shower. The water was so hot it was almost at a boiling point but it felt good. He could hardly bring himself to get out. He checked the windows to see if anyone was around, then he threw his clothes in the dryer and then went to set his homemade alarms. He then grabbed a pillow and quilt and curled up on the floor behind the couch. It had been a long and stressful night. He wondered what the cops knew. He saw them find the body and saw the coroner's van. Did they suspect it was him or someone else? Did they think it was an accident or a murder? The only thing he knew for sure was it was time to go and he had to do it tonight.

Frank and Shelly slept like the dead. All the while they were gone to I-Hop, the police department was busy trying to find out what they could about the body they had found. As soon as they got back to the department with the crudely taken fingerprints they had gotten at the scene, they ran them through the system. They had already ran the prints from the hand and it had found a match only minutes ago. The prints came back to a Jared Greenly from Missouri. He had a record of driving with a suspended license in 2007, and he had his license revoked from DWI's or driving while intoxicated from that year, and two more in 2008. That might account for the lack of identification on his body, assuming that it was the one the hand belonged to.

While they read the printout on the prints of the hand

while the prints from the body were running, the computer beeped out a sound that made all of the officers turn to look at the screen. They already had a match for the prints from the body, and as suspected, they were the same as the hand.

"Well, you know what you have to do now. The Sergeant said to the officer that had already been notified that he would be the one making the trip to Little Rock to reunite the hand with its body. He turned back toward the rest of the officers and started giving out orders. I want someone to get on the phone and find out if he has next of kin in Missouri and notify them that we have a body that we believe to be his, and ask them if they know why he might have been in Arkansas. Tell them that the body will be returned here once the Crime Lab is done and then they can make funeral arrangements to ship the body. He turned to someone else and asked them to run a check on missing persons in the system and see if Jared Greenly's name or photo came up.

While he had everyone working on those things, he radioed the other officers on patrol to give them the news. It was almost time for his shift to be over and he made himself a note to get back in touch with the couple, Frank and Shelly, who were staying at the Hills and Holler's cabin resort to let them know what they had found out and ask if they had seen anything else.

The only news he got before going off shift, was that one officer had finally gotten in touch with Jared Greenly's parents. They were obviously upset at the news but at the same time, didn't seem surprised to hear it. They explained that they had not been in touch with him in over two years and that he had been hitch-hiking the country after losing his license and then his job. He had just stopped caring and made money wherever he could any way he could and would spend it on alcohol if he ever made any money. They said they would leave as soon as it was daylight and drive down as they had trouble driving in the dark. It would be over a seven hour drive for them one way. The officer told them that they didn't have to come down to identify the body since they fingerprints had already confirmed who it was, and that the decomposition was so bad that it would be hard, if not impossible to identify someone in that condition. They said they understood and thanked him for trying to spare them the trouble and for trying to prevent them from any more pain that anything they would see might cause them. They explained that even though they hadn't seen Jared in two years that it was only right to come and be with the body of their son. They would arrange a hearse with their local funeral home to follow them and pick up his body and they would follow it back home. After hearing that news, the Sergeant gave his shift report to the supervisor on the next shift and he went home to get some rest.

    Morning and noon had already passed and it was almost 3pm before Frank and Shelly opened their eyes. They were disoriented and knew they had overslept but was shocked to look at the time on the alarm clock. They both showered and dressed and met downstairs on the couch to put on their tennis shoes.

    "Wow, what a night!" Shelly said first.

    "You're telling me." Frank agreed.

Deciding they could wait until later to check on the cabins since they did that when they first came in that morning, Frank and Shelly drove up to a fast food restaurant and went inside. With an ulterior motive, they ordered a cup of coffee for the both of them and they sat down at one of the booths near the window closest to the street. Shelly opened up her laptop and began to e-mail their family and friends using the restaurant's Wi-Fi while they slowly sipped on the hot java. If they called everyone with the same story it would take until next week, and this way she could send a blanket e-mail to explain everything and not have to spend time on the phone. She had to think a minute, but finally realized it was Saturday and they had one week left of their vacation. They had done so much in the few days that they had been there and had enjoyed every minute of it, up until last night, but even as she thought this, she decided that even last night was kind of fun in a twisted sort of way. It was exciting to say the least and something they would never forget and would enjoy telling everyone. She laughed as she told Frank what she was thinking and he laughed along with her.

They sat inside the restaurant and enjoyed just sitting there and not actually having an agenda for the day and just relaxing. They had been on the move ever since they got there and it was nice doing nothing. They took their time drinking the coffee and sending e-mails. They caught up on reading a few they had gotten during the week as well.

"Do you miss it yet?" Frank was looking intently at Shelly as he asked the question.

"Miss what?"

"Home...our busy lives...the city?"

"No. She said without hesitation. Do you?"

"No. He answered. I really have enjoyed it here. The small town life. The beauty of all the places we've seen. Slowing down, and just being with you."

She leaned over and kissed Frank softly on the cheek. It was a sweet thing for him to say and as she thought about it, she really hadn't missed their normal lives in the least. Not that she hated what they did or where they lived, she just hadn't missed it. This just felt like another world and she was comfortable in it.

They got done eating and dumped their trash in the trash bin by the door and walked out to Cecil's truck. They were so used to it that it almost felt like they owned it. Frank laughed as he put the key into the keyhole in the door to unlock it, something in their whole lives they hadn't had to do. Every vehicle they had owned had an automatic door unlock on their key chain or "key fob" as they were sometimes called. They laughed at some of the things they had seen since they got to Mountain View. The old well outside their cabin that had the sweet spring water. The hand pump in the kitchen. They had seen houses here that did not have central heat and air, or even a chimney, but an old stove pipe coming from the roof of the house. This town didn't have a car rental and even the Walmart didn't stay open all night. There was no all-night pharmacy and it was also a dry county. Cell phones did not work in some places. Still, it was nice and they almost felt like regulars now.

They decided that they would just stay in that night

and buy a few movies to watch and cook their own meal later in the evening of spaghetti. They went to Walmart to grab the few items they would need to make it, and some extra drinks. It was still a little early to go back to the cabin and watch the movies when they got out of the store, so they decided to drive around the town some more. They went from one end to the other and side to side. There were little places they remembered that just felt good to see again and then things they saw that they hadn't noticed the other times they had been out.

"There's the little church that the couple sitting next to us at the Court Square invited us to on Sunday morning! Shelly exclaimed.

"Well, it is. Frank said. Would you like to go?"

"I think I might. She said with her head tilted to one side. I know that neither one of our families are very religious, but I do remember going with my grandparents when I was little and it was nice. I've always believed in God, but just haven't pursued going to church like I have my career."

"I know what you mean. Frank stated. I've always believed too, in fact that's why I wouldn't get married to you in front of a justice of the peace because I'm around law and court every day and there's nothing "just" or even "peaceful" about it sometimes. It seems like when you get married in a church it's like God is there too. So, we can go in the morning and then figure out what else to do tomorrow."

Someone's Watching

Chapter12

They finished their drive around town and then headed back toward their cabin. They would do all of the door checks on each of the cabins early and go back and watch their movies and cook spaghetti later.

****

The Mountain View police had changed shifts at 6PM and the same officers that were on the night before, during the finding of the hand and body, were on again. The day shift had passed on some information to them to call the State Crime Lab for some new information they had about the blood samples from the yard. The Sergeant made the call and waited as the forensics technician explained that the blood samples from every place they had collected, was in fact human blood, and to make it more interesting, the blood matched that of the body that had been brought in. They were still working on determining cause of death, as they had had a pretty full case load the night before and they hadn't gotten to the body yet, but would in a few hours.

The Sergeant thanked them and hung up the phone calling an impromptu meeting of every officer on duty. He informed them of the new information he had received and when he got to the part about the blood matching the body they had found in the ditch he added; "and you know what that means...it means that he was most likely killed there in front of the office and then moved to that ditch, in my opinion, to make it look like an accident. Somebody killed the man and that is a homicide. We need to start looking for a murderer, whether it is someone local, or even those people renting the cabins, even though I don't think they had anything to do with it. There's no way to check an alibi for them because they are staying there alone and we don't the exact time of death, and cause of death. We don't even know what weapon, if any, was used. I'm going to go out there and question them some more. I'm not going to interrogate them though, after all, they were the ones who brought our attention to the hand in the first place, so my gut says they are not the guilty party. Last but not least, we still have to think about this serial killer. It could just be him. Hard to believe, here in Mountain View, but it could be him. Find out if anyone has made a report of any stolen weapons, vehicles or anything in the last week. Let's get going!"

Everyone fanned out in different directions, each knowing which task would be theirs from doing it before in different circumstances on different cases. The Sergeant included.

The first thing the Sergeant did was to get in his car and head towards the cabins to talk to Frank and Shelly. While he was driving he was thinking. It was a puzzle to him why someone would be killed there in that place. No one else was there but Frank and Shelly, and again, he didn't think they had anything to do with it. If they had, then why would they have brought attention to themselves about the hand? It could be someone local that had gotten mad at the man for whatever reason, and had killed him in a fit of rage. If it was the serial killer, then where was he? No one had reported seeing a suspicious person. Frank and Shelly hadn't seen anyone while they were staying there, unless they just hadn't seen him. Maybe he had been there, but they just didn't see him? With all of these thoughts it was worth checking out. As soon as he got to the resort he would explain it to them. He was almost to the turn off when he saw the old truck they had been driving parked at a gas station getting gas. He pulled in behind them.

At first they seemed startled until they saw who it was and they shook hands when he approached. While Frank pumped the gas into Cecil's old truck, the Sergeant told them about the news and asked if he could go along with them and do a more thorough check of the place. They were appreciative of that and were more than happy to have them accompany them. When they were done, they headed off down the hill towards the cabins.

As they pulled up into the office parking lot, the Sergeant radioed his dispatch to let them know his location and that he was going to do a property check with the caretakers of the Hills and Hollers cabin rentals. He stepped out of his patrol car and locked it, with the keys in his hand. Frank and Shelly did the same with the truck.

They informed him that the only key they didn't have was the key to the office and that it had been locked every day they had checked it. They all walked around the building to the rear and back again. The Sergeant peering in through the windows at the desk and computers. He walked past the woodpile on the front porch and looked off of the end and walked back. Not sure what he was looking for or that he was looking for anything in particular he continued on toward the opposite end and did the same. Finally, not seeing anything out of order, they got back in their vehicles and continued on to the next cabin. Maybe he would find a clue at one of those since Frank and Shelly said they had the master key to all of them.

The Contemporary Cabin was the first one on the way back. The patrol car was following behind the truck closely. Michael Delacroix was sitting out in the woods grateful that he had gotten up and gotten out of it when he did, and cleaned everything back to its original state. After having the shower and some sleep, he felt like a new man and had been able to eat something when he woke up, the nausea finally gone with the smell gone.

He wondered what the police were doing out here now. They had already hauled off the body and there were no more hands to be found. Maybe they didn't trust the couple and thought they were responsible? Maybe they thought there might be another body? Or, he thought, maybe they were looking for him. That thought made his heart beat faster and his breath quicken. If that was the case, then he hoped that every cabin he had been in looked unused. He had always made a point of checking, but there could always be something he missed.

He watched as the officer, a Sergeant, got out of his car. He could see that he took his keys and locking the cruiser, followed the couple to the door. They tried the lock and it was locked, of course, but then they actually took the master key, and for the first time, went inside. They were in there about ten minutes when they finally came out with no obvious expression on their faces and got into their vehicles and drove off. He assumed they would do this with every place. He debated on whether or not to follow them or to stay where he was. He would be curious about whether they had noticed anything at any of the other places, but he would never be sure since he couldn't hear them, and also, if he moved every time they did, they might notice him out in the woods or hear him. It would also waste a lot of his energy. He decided to stay put. He would be nervous the whole time but would wait and be ready for anything. He hoped that the rest of the police department didn't descend on the property as well and have another search.

It was almost two hours before he saw the patrol car coming back down the winding gravel road and pass the spot where he sat out in the woods. It was getting dark now and he was glad for the cover it provided as he made his way toward the last cabin on the road.

He would take his time and sit and study the cabin and try to tell what was going on inside. His plan might not go perfectly well, because there *was* no exact plan, but one way or another, he would get those keys to the truck and he would leave tonight. If he didn't have to kill them, then the truck would be gone before the next morning. If he *did* have to kill them, the truck would be gone and they would also be in it. That way, the police would just think they were gone somewhere or that they had stolen the truck themselves and left for good.

While Frank and Shelly and the Sergeant looked and checked through each cabin, he told them about the new developments they had found out. He explained that the hand did belong to the body. Frank and Shelly were not surprised that it matched and was a little relieved that it did because that meant that there wasn't someone else missing a hand... or a life.

While they were talking, the police department radioed him and told him that the officer he had assigned to get in touch with Jared Greenly's parents had indeed spoken with them. The officer wanted to let his Sergeant know that the deceased subject had been a hitchhiker or drifter according to his parents. That explained why he was here in Arkansas. It still didn't explain why he had been killed on the cabin grounds and by whom.

They noticed the Sergeant had asked them several more questions about where they had been in the last few days and they knew the reason why and wanted to help clear themselves and ease his mind. Shelly had an idea and told him that they had taken hundreds of photos with their digital cameras. She explained that when you take a photo with it, the camera itself stores its own information about the date and time the photo was taken. She told him that when they got to their cabin, she would show him the camera, which still had all of the photos on the micro SD card and let him write down the dates and times that they were gone and by the photos, he could see where and when they had been at any particular place. He was impressed by her idea and wanted to see the photos. It would not eliminate every hour that they were able

to be accounted for, but it was something to help show that they were on vacation and not here to stalk and kill unsuspecting victims.

When they finally got to their cabin and showed him the photos, he was impressed with not only the times and dates of the pictures, but the subject matter of the photos as well, and told them that they were very good photographers and that their photos should be sold as calendars or in magazines or hanging in the hallways of buildings such as hospitals or other businesses. Frank laughed shyly and said that as a matter of fact, several were in New York in the law office where he worked and a few other places in town that had been gracious enough to want to buy them.

The Sergeant congratulated them and said if they ever decided to quit the jobs that they had, they could make a good living as professional photographers. They thanked him and he got back to business. The search of the cabins didn't turn up anything of proof that anyone had been there. The only thing they found were some used soap wrappers and food wrappers in the trash cans, which were normal, so he finally turned to leave and said to give the police department a call if they found anything else. He said he would still have an officer patrol their cabin resort grounds a couple of times a night, and with that, he was gone.

After the Sergeant left, they put up their groceries and settled in for a long evening of movies and food. This was just as exciting to them as going out and doing something. They had gotten four movies and it was only 5PM so they would have plenty of time to watch all of them and take a break to cook.

They weren't tired or sleepy after having slept so late in the day and they were ready to enjoy themselves.

Frank built a fire and Shelly rounded up all of the blankets and pillows and threw them on the big oversized couch. They got all of the movies and placed them on the coffee table. Frank closed his eyes as Shelly mixed them up and had him to put his finger down on the one they would watch first. He opened his eyes and was happy to see he had chosen a comedy they had bought. That would be good to start the night out with. They popped it in and took their places on the couch and started watching, even letting the previews play all the way through.

Neither one of them could remember ever having this much time to themselves since they had gotten married. Even before, for that matter. Frank was just finishing up college and Shelly was just starting her own business when they tied the knot. Since their honeymoon, which they'd been very busy trying to see and do all that they could on their trip to Vegas, they really hadn't had a chance to relax for this amount of time.

The movie, true to its label, was definitely a comedy and Frank and Shelly were in tears within the first few minutes from laughing so hard. It was a simple story in which the main character was just clumsy and got everything wrong and created problems wherever he went due to his inability to get anything right. Every situation was full of hilarious mishaps that were very easily a possibility to happen. Frank and Shelly talked about how this was a movie like they would've made back in the 1980's when comedy was actually funny and not dark and malicious like the movies being produced today. Nothing was even funny in comedies anymore and they wondered if it was because every storyline that was possibly funny had already been used or was it because every character in every movie spewed vile, filthy language for a situation that was less than comedic due to the screen writers lack of ability to create anything funny in this day and time.

When the movie was finally over, their sides hurt so bad from laughing that they had to wait for a few minutes before getting up to do anything. They would recommend that movie to everyone. Finally starting to get hungry, they decided to cook their spaghetti and cheesy garlic bread. They got up from the couch and went into the kitchen to prepare their gourmet meal.

They both enjoyed cooking and wished they had more time at home to do so. It was hard to work all day and then come home and cook a meal, so they usually just did take out or grabbed something on the way home to eat. They also had healthy microwaveable meals and steamers that were good, but nothing compared to something you cooked yourself. The cabin was filled with the aroma of spaghetti sauce and hamburger meat mixed with the smell of the cheesy garlic bread.

While the spaghetti was boiling, Frank went out on the porch to get a few more sticks of fire wood. Even though it was May, it was still a little cool at night here in the "hills and hollers" of Mountain View and the fireplace put out just the right amount of heat to make it cozy and not hot. As he stepped out onto the porch he could smell the fresh country night air and breathed in deep. He gathered his arms full of sticks of wood and went back into the cabin. He put a few onto the crackling fire and neatly stacked the rest on the hearth. That should last the rest of the night.

The spaghetti was done and Shelly was putting it in a strainer and asked Frank to take the garlic bread out of the oven. Shelly added some butter to the steaming noodles and a few heaping spoonful's of hamburger meat to each bowl she had put the noodles in and then dipped a generous amount of sauce over that. Frank handed her some toast and put a piece on his plate as well. They fixed a couple of glasses of soft drinks and carried their meal over to the coffee table to eat while they watched another movie. This time it was an action movie.

They both went back for seconds and were so engrossed in the movie that they didn't hear the knock on their door and jumped when they finally heard the pounding.

"Mountain View Police Department."

Frank jumped over to the door to unlock it and let them in.

"Hello..I'm Officer Smith. We're doing extra patrols of this area and the resort here and just wanted to check on you and see if everything was ok."

Frank laughed and told him that he had scared them because they had been watching movies and didn't hear him drive up. He assured the officer that they were fine and thanked him for checking on them. He asked if there had been any new developments. The officer said that there hadn't, but would let them know if there was anything they needed to be aware of. After a few more words the officer told Frank that he would be back later on and check on the, but wouldn't knock on the door and wake them. Frank thanked him and Officer Smith turned and went back to his car.

They had had so much fun the whole day that the night before seemed long ago and far away, except when they really thought about it, and they had finally gotten over their fear that they'd had after finding the hand and the body. It made them feel even better to know that the police department was still checking in on them and they relaxed again and settled back in to finish their movie.

****

He had just watched the patrol car drive up and the officer get out and talk to the couple in the cabin, and then drive off. He wondered what he talked to them about. He was surprised they were still talking to them. Maybe they had a few more questions to ask them. Anyway, the officer was gone now and he could relax a little.

He had been sitting out there all evening and it was probably close to 10PM by now and the couple seemed to be making a night of watching TV or movies. The only thing he had seen them do is cook and come out for fire wood. He could smell the food and it made him hungry.

It was a little cool out in the woods and he was cold, but it kept him sharp. He had gotten used to staying in the cabins and that made a night like this harder.

Hopefully he wouldn't have to be out there too much longer.

****

The next movie they watched was a horror movie. They had saved a romantic love story for last to get their mind off of anything too scary so they could sleep. It was a "Zombie" movie that looked so real that they could almost believe it was possible or happening right then. The characters did a great job of being believable and the zombies themselves deserved academy awards for their own acting despite not have to say anything intelligible but moaning. Frank and Shelly gave it a five star rating as they put in the last movie and ran to take bathroom breaks. It was now midnight and the day was finally winding down for them. After this last one it would be time for bed. Shelly had to have a snack of chocolate chip cookies and milk and Frank had a bowl of cereal.

Hour after hour they watched movies in the downstairs living room. Michael Delacroix wished he had been closer so he could've watched them too. When his stomach started growling so loud he was afraid they would hear it above their show, he reached into the bag of food he had accumulated from the cabins and ate several crackers with peanut butter. He only had one bottle of water with him, and with his mouth so puckered from the peanut butter, he drank the whole thing. He decided that eating the snack was a good idea because he

didn't need to be hungry doing what he had to do tonight. He needed to have all of his focus on the task at hand.

****

The romantic movie had been a sweet and happy movie, ending in the main characters getting married to the love of their life. It was 2:30AM when they finally turned the

TV off, checked the door locks and hit the lights as they went upstairs to bed.

As they crawled under the covers together and Shelly fell into place, her head on Frank's shoulder with his arm around her, they talked about what a fun day it had been. It was just like when they were dating and went out to do fun stuff all of the time. It was, in fact, just like they were teenagers having the time of their lives. Each day had been a new adventure and they still had another week to go before they went back home. Shelly groaned at the word "work" and Frank hugged her and reminded her that even though they were going back to work at the jobs they truly loved, they still had the rest of their lives to have new adventures and wouldn't stop having them even when they got old. Shelly raised up on one elbow and kissed Frank deeply and passionately for such a loving comment. After that, it was a while before they finally went to sleep happily in each other's arms.

****

Finally the lights were out. He watched as the light upstairs went on briefly and then it went out too. Good. They were in bed. It was time to start counting the minutes. Another good hour and then whatever happened, happened.

Fight For Your Life
Chapter 13

    Michael Delacroix tried to be calm but his nerves were getting the best of him. The more he tried to calm himself down, the more excited he got. Soon he would be on the road in a truck. He hoped that it had plenty of gas and then it worried him that it might not have. While he was in there, he might try to get the girl's purse or the man's wallet. It all depended on what happened. If he had to kill them, then it would be no problem to get those things. If he could get by without having to, then he would have a harder job to do. No doubt the keys were probably in the same area as the wallet.

    It was pitch black outside tonight. The moon, only a crescent, showed little light. That was better for him so that he could slip around without being seen as easily, and speaking of that, the thought reminded him that he needed to go disable the phone line at the side of the cabin. All of the cabins had one or two phones in them and he wouldn't want them making a 911 call in case things didn't go right.

All of the thoughts had been going over and over in his mind like a checklist of things to do. He had rehearsed this night so many times that he felt as if he had already lived through it in a past life and was reliving it again. He knew it was almost time and he could feel the palms of his hands get sweaty as his adrenaline started to flow. He slowly stood from his crouched position and stretched his legs and swung his arms like a marathon runner about to begin a race. He took a couple of deep breaths and began his Natural State escape.

He doubted he would need the bag of food any longer, but it might come in handy if he didn't have any money and got hungry. He slipped over to the back of the truck and quietly placed it in the truck bed on the driver's side. The peanut butter was heavy enough that it wouldn't blow out and he had it tied tight at the top. The tools he had used over a dozen times to let himself into each cabin was in the top of the overalls so he could grab them easily. First though, he had to get to that phone line.

He sprinted in the darkness across front yard of the cabin and into the shadows on the side. He wished he had a flashlight. He would have to feel for the wire. He ran his hands over the rounded logs sweeping them from side to side until the tips of his fingers hit something. He stopped and examined it more closely and knew that this was what he was feeling for. He followed it down until he found the box and then working his fingers under the wire until he could get his whole hand under it, closed them around it and gave a hard jerk, popping it loose from the connection it had in the box. He was breathing heavy and fast, so with that done, he stood still for a moment listening to make sure no one heard and came out to investigate.

Everything was silent except a slight breeze blowing through the trees. He had been cold before, but now he could feel the perspiration on his skin and the breeze felt good. He stood there a minute longer getting up his nerve and then he slipped around the side of the house and up onto the porch. He leaned over at the front door to the lock, and trying it first, on the off chance that it might not be locked, sighed ever so slightly to find that it was. He quickly reached up to the front pocket of the coveralls for the piece of wire and the nail. It didn't take him more than fifteen seconds to have the door unlocked. He put his tools back in their pocket on his chest and pushed the door open ever so slightly.

It was dark inside the cabin and quiet. He stepped inside and carefully closed the door until it was only open a crack. Trying to let his eyes get adjusted to the darkness he stood there looking around for objects so that he wouldn't trip over them. He had made it over to the couch and knew there was a table at one end with a lamp and a coffee table in front of the couch. He got to the end table first and felt around with his hands. Nothing there. His eyes steadily getting used to the dark and more able to make out shapes, noticed a square shaped object on the coffee table. Could it actually be the wallet? He put his hand on top of it and felt the smooth worn leather beneath his fingers, and not only that, the truck keys were beneath it! This meant he wouldn't have to kill the couple. God had made another way for him to get their vehicle without harming them in the process. He was so excited he almost didn't hear the flush of the toilet about twelve steps away.

He grabbed both wallet and keys and dove for the kitchen hoping to escape unseen, but in the process of diving, he hadn't accounted for an unseen object in the way and collided into it with a crash. His cover blown, he slid over to the utensil drawer and scrambled for a knife, finding it just as the lights came on. He was on his feet and ready to defend

himself and now that he had been seen, the choice had been made, by God he figured. He had to kill them.

****

Frank stood there frozen for a second bewildered and then scared. There was a very large man in the kitchen and he had a knife. Franks wallet and keys lay on the kitchen floor at his feet.

"You're not going to win." The man said.

Frank, knowing that he was smaller in bulk and in stature than the man, but being used to the intimidating types in court, knew that he had at least better call his bluff. He was by no means a fighter, but he was in good shape and wasn't the type to back down and give in, especially if he was fighting for his life, and for Shelly's this time. He stepped over toward the fireplace and grabbed the fireplace poker off of the hearth.

"I promise...you'll lose. The last guy did." The man said to intimidate him, then added; I believe you found his hand a couple of days ago."

"Yeah, did you try to steal his keys and wallet too?" Frank asked sarcastically.

"No. He didn't have keys or a wallet. He was just chosen. Like you are."

Puzzled at what the man had said, Frank began to think and then it dawned on him who he was.

"You're the serial killer that escaped from that prison close to here aren't you." Frank asked.

"Yes. I am."

Figuring that it was no point in debating the issue of why he was "chosen" with a crazy man, Frank inched forward with the poker. The look on the serial killer's face was one of surprise mixed with a twisted proud astonishment. Frank knew it was a bold move, but he wasn't about to show fear.

"Why don't you take the money out of my wallet, and take the keys and be on your way to wherever it is you're going and not put us both through this." Frank suggested knowing what the answer would be.

"Can't do that. It don't work that way." He answered with a serious look while shaking his head.

"O.K." Frank countered lowering his chin and staring hard at the serial killer. "We'll do it your way. You'll have to come and get me."

With a long deep laugh, the serial killer bent his head and charged full tilt like a bull towards a matador, the knife held in his fist and out to the side. Frank had time to swing, but with him coming at him from a forward position and bent over with his head down, it was hard to deliver a solid blow and the momentum knocked him over sideways.

Shelly had been sound asleep when Frank had gotten up to go to the bathroom. Suddenly she was awake and not sure why. Had something crashed or gotten broken in the cabin somewhere? She lay still and listened. Frank was not in bed with her. Could he have fallen? She started to call out to him and then she heard voices. One was Frank's and the other one was of another man. They weren't loud enough to hear what they were saying and she thought perhaps it might be another police officer stopping by to check on them, but then remembered that the officer earlier had said that he wouldn't wake them and she thought that he might've had some news that they really needed to hear, or that he had seen a light on and figured it was ok. That's when she noticed that the light was indeed on and Frank usually never turned on the light just to go to the bathroom. Then she heard the crash and scuffling noises and leapt out of bed to see what was happening.

She looked over the loft railing and saw Frank and another larger man rolling on the floor in the living room. Her first thought was to scream, but she didn't want to put Frank in more danger, so she covered her mouth with her hand.

The phone! She needed to call 911. She grabbed her cell phone from the nightstand and dialed the number. It wouldn't go through. She had forgotten about the bad cell phone service here. There was the regular cabin phone on Frank's side of the bed. She quietly went over to it and dialed it again. No sound. The lines had been cut? The man fighting with Frank must have done it. Thoughts were racing through her head of why would someone do that to them and that they must've known what they were doing if they had thought to do that and then it hit her. The serial killer! She gasped as fear paralyzed her at the thought of the hand they had seen and the body the police department had found. He was trying to kill Frank and if he killed Frank he would kill her too. She had to do something.

Thinking hard she scrambled over to her duffel bag and dug through it quickly until she found what she was looking for. She finally felt it at the bottom and closed her fingers around it. It was a can of police grade pepper spray that some friends of theirs from Frank's law firm, who were also friends with the local NYPD, had given them to help keep them safe walking the streets of New York. It was supposed to be much stronger than commercial grade pepper spray.

Now, how was she going to use it? It sure wouldn't be in the nightgown she had on. She quickly grabbed the pair of jeans on the floor she'd stripped off when they had gone to bed and slipped them on. Then throwing the nightgown off over her head, she put on a t-shirt. She was ready to do battle. Her only regret was not having her tennis shoes on, but they were downstairs by the door.

She crept over to the railing and eased a look down onto the floor below. They were fighting!

Frank hit the serial killer with the poker, but his momentum had thrown him off balance and he fell over sideways onto the coffee table, knocking the poker out of his hand. The serial killer had taken a blow that had seemed to slow him, but for only seconds before he was ready to attack again. Frank reached over and grabbed the poker and was trying to propel himself up from the floor before the killer got to him, but he didn't have enough time. The killer caught him just as he was standing, and slashed his shoulder with the knife, knocking Frank to the floor again. The poker landing a few feet behind him. With the knife still in the killer's hand, Frank reached backwards and grabbed the poker again and hit the killer on top of the shoulder with it. It wasn't a very hard hit and the killer grabbed the poker and threw it sideways and lunged forward toward Frank with the knife. Frank rolled to the side. He lunged again and Frank caught his hands and was desperately trying to hold him off but the knife was just inches from his throat and the killer's body weight was heavy and pressing down on him. He could feel his shoulder burning and tingling and could tell he was losing strength in that arm and his whole body felt weak.

All of a sudden, from behind the killer's head, Shelly appeared and thrust something right in front of the killer's face and he began to cough and sputter, still clutching the knife in one hand and trying to wipe his eyes with the other, coughing and gasping for breath. He jumped to his feet and began running blindly for the kitchen sink. He was still coughing and gasping as he found it.

Shelly rushed over to Frank who, for some reason, was still lying on the floor.

"Frank, we have to run! She said frantically. Get up!"

"I'm so weak I can't move. Frank said looking at her with fear in his eyes. That's when Shelly noticed the blood. It was all over the floor and pooling all around Frank. She looked at his shoulder and it was sliced all the way to the bone and spurting. He had sliced through an artery and Frank was losing blood fast.

Shelly didn't have time to talk. She ripped off her shirt and put it around Franks arm and tied it as tight as she could, praying that she could do it before the killer got his eyes washed out enough to see again. She took a quick look back and saw he still had his head under the faucet. She told Frank that she loved him and not to move and to hold on. She knew what she had to do and she had to do it now. If she didn't they would never make it out alive. Frank might not still.

Still praying, she jumped up and ran across the room and grabbed the poker. She gripped it tight in her hands and pulled her arms close to her body and took a deep breath and began to run straight at the killer's body.

Shelly hit him with such impact that at first she thought she'd missed him. He stopped washing his face and stood up straight and stiff. Shelly let go of the poker and looked down. It was sticking through his back and she couldn't see the end of it. Then he started to turn with a low growl. Shelly started backing away wondering where she had dropped the pepper spray. He had made the turn and was facing her, the end of the poker sticking out through his stomach. It was a horrible sight and terrifying because he still kept walking toward her, slowly and deliberately. She was still frantically searching for the pepper spray.

Finally she saw it had roller under the edge of the couch. She threw herself down on the floor and reached up under it with her arm. He was only two steps away as she finally reached the can. She curled her fingers around it and sat up, quickly aiming again for his face, when she heard the shots…Pow…Pow…Pow!

It was the Officer Smith. He was standing in the doorway with his weapon drawn, still aiming at the serial killer. Shelly turned back to look at the killer and was amazed that he still stood there, but could tell that he was losing composure. He had a defeated look on his face that was almost sad. He coughed and blood poured from his mouth. He fell to his knees and then said; "I'm sorry for what I've done. He could hardly get the last words out as he sputtered: "Please bury me by my mother." Then he slumped forward, arms limp with his head down, still in the sitting position on his knees, the poker sticking straight out behind him. He was dead.

The officer, seeing that Frank was injured, reached up to his radio and called for an ambulance "now!" and stepped over to help Shelly any way he could. Shelly was holding pressure on Frank's arm and asked the officer to raise his feet up in the air.

Frank was still conscious but very weak and his pulse was getting faster. He told Shelly that he loved her and thanked her for doing what she did. He was proud of her. She cried while he talked to her telling him not to talk, but cherishing every word that he said to her.

Finally the ambulance arrived and the EMT's ran in with their medical equipment and started two I.V's with them running wide open. Then they put a blood pressure cuff over the shirt that Shelly had tied on Frank's arm, and inflated it as tight as they could without it popping off. One of the EMT's went to get the cot while the other one gathered up their equipment so they could go. When the EMT came back in with the cot, he also brought a long spine board so they could put Frank on the stretcher more easily. The officer let his feet down and assisted them in log rolling him onto the long spine board and lifting him up onto the cot.

As they rolled him out to the ambulance, the officer held the I.V. bags and upon their instruction, and squeezed them as tight as he could, forcing more fluid into the patient at a faster rate. He finally let go when the paramedic got in the back and took over. He said he would be over to the hospital as soon as he could, but would have to take care of the matter at the cabin and wait on the coroner.

The paramedic allowed Shelly to ride in the back of the ambulance. The EMT shut the doors and jumped back in the cab and took off at lightning speed, lights ablaze and siren wailing as soon as they pulled out onto the highway.

On the way there the paramedic asked Shelly to keep the cuff inflated to 300mmHg on the blood pressure cuff's dial by squeezing the bulb occasionally when it went down. The paramedic stood and squeezed one of the I.V. bags continuously, the other hand keying up the mic, while giving his radio report to the hospital. Frank's pressure was still dangerously low, and just before they got to the hospital, the paramedic spiked another bag of fluid. He squeezed it until the EMT backed up and opened the doors of the ambulance to a waiting team of medical personnel that was standing on the ambulance bay.

As they wheeled Frank into the emergency room Shelly went to give his information to the receptionist so everything would go more smoothly and any blood or tests they ordered wouldn't be delayed because they didn't have his information. She hated to be away from him, but it was necessary and she didn't think they would want her back there while they were doing everything they had to do.

When she was done answering all of the questions they had, a tech came and got her and showed her where to sit in the waiting room and said a nurse would come and talk to her soon. While she waited, a couple of the police officers came and stayed with her, not bothering her about the details of what happened yet.

In a few minutes the charge nurse came out and told her that they had given Frank some blood and had brought his pressure back up, but that he would have to go to the O.R. to have the arterial bleed fixed, and would be going in just a couple of minutes. They allowed her to go in and talk to him before he went. He was barely conscious and had been given some medication and was groggy. Shelly kissed him and told him she loved him and would see him as soon as he got out of surgery.

After they wheeled him away, she went back out and sat down with the officers. She was glad they were there. It was a comfort to know that somebody cared about them because without Frank there, she was all alone. For the first time since it all happened, she cried.

One of the officers put his arm around her and just held her. The tech brought her a box of tissues. When she finally regained composure she thanked the officer and then thanked both of them for just being there. They told her that it was their jobs and that's what they do, but she knew they had gone above their job duties to be nice.

They walked back to the waiting area and one of the officers got her a cup of coffee. They sat down and she explained their

whole evening and what happened with the serial killer. When she said the words "serial killer" she stopped and asked; "It was him wasn't it?"

"Yes ma'am...it seems that way. We have his photo from the BOLO or be on the lookout photo we got over ACIC and it's him." The older officer explained.

"Looks like he was in a world of hurt before our officer shot him!" The younger officer said with a grin.

Shelly smiled in spite of the situation and then sighed and told them she simply did what she had to do to survive and to keep Frank alive.

"Well, I'd say you did an excellent job. If you would like to join our department at any time, please stop by and fill out an application. We could use more people like you."

They were still talking when Officer Smith finally got there. He said the coroner had just taken the body away. He told Shelly that the crime scene photos had already been taken and the scene had been processed. He found the keys to the cabin and had locked it up, and had been gracious enough to bring them to her, along with Frank's wallet and her purse as well. She thanked him as tears ran down her face at the sentiment.

"Well, if you're anything like my wife, a woman never leaves home without her purse. The officer said smiling. I knew you didn't have time to get it earlier."

After answering several questions he needed for his report about what had happened before he arrived at the

cabin he told her to try and relax. That everything was going to be alright now and they would be checking on them later.

Recovery

Chapter 14

He and the other officers left and Shelly was finally truly alone. She only wished the officer had gotten her cell phone so she could call their families. Looking down into her purse, she was surprised to see Frank's cell lying at the bottom of it and then remembered that he had tossed it in there when they had gone driving around the day before and had forgotten to take it out while they were watching movies and plug it up on the charger. It only had a little bit of battery power left, so she called Frank's parents first, and then her own. Not going into as much graphic detail as she could have, to make it quick enough so the battery would last, she skimmed through exactly what happened and just gave them the bare bones.

"There was a serial killer loose, he wound up at our cabin and tried to kill us. Frank got slashed with a knife and had an arterial bleed in his arm and is in surgery. I'm waiting to hear from the doctor. They think he'll do fine." Was about all she could say because the phone started beeping its low battery signal.

She could tell everyone was horrified at the news, but relieved that Frank should be fine and that she didn't get hurt. Before the cell went dead, she promised them she would call as soon as Frank came out of surgery one way or the other.

With the phone dead and no one to talk to, she prayed to God to let Frank make it alright during the surgery, and grateful that they survived the horrible encounter, she gave thanks as well.

It had been over two hours since Frank had been wheeled in to the operating room. It was now close to 6AM and finally the doors opened and the doctor stepped out. Shelly jumped up from her seat to see how it went.

"Are you Shelly?" He asked as she nodded answering.

"Your husband came through surgery fine, but he had a very bad cut. It completely severed the artery and probably got some nerves. He had lost a significant amount of blood as well, and we had to give him four units of blood."

Shelly had covered her mouth while she was listening, eyes wide and tearful. "Is he going to be ok? She asked. Will he be able to use his arm normally?"

"Yes, he'll recover just fine. The arm will be weak and he will probably have some numbness and tingling in one or more places that may or may not go away with time. After a few weeks he may want to start using some very light weights, like five pounds or so and then work up from that to get his strength back in it. In a couple of months, it should be much better. He will have several stitches that will have to be removed in ten days and he will need to wear a sling for two or three weeks, but he will be fine."

Shelly breathed a sigh of relief and thanked the doctor for letting her know and for taking care of him during surgery.

"He needs to stay in here overnight and maybe one more day to make sure nothing goes wrong, such as a leak or a reaction to the blood transfusion, and he still needs to be on I.V. and have antibiotics to prevent an infection. Do you have any more questions?"

"Can I see him?" She asked

"The nurses are about to move him to a room in just a few minutes and you can follow them to it." He said smiling.

Shelly thanked him again and waited on Frank to come rolling out. Five minutes later he did.

He looked so very frail and delicate lying there in his hospital gown with bandages on his arm and an I.V. in his arm. He was still asleep from the medication and she decided not to wake him until they got to the room. She followed behind the nurses as they rolled him down the hallway. When they got to the room and finished getting his bed in place, one of the nurses asked if she needed anything. Shelly explained about not having a charged battery on Frank's cell phone and was there a way she could make an out of state call and charge it to her credit card. The nurse told her they could do better than that, and got the hospital chaplain to use a long distance calling code and have it billed to the hospital so she could talk to both of their families. Shelly was grateful. The nurse said just to wait on the chaplain in the room with Frank and he would be there soon.

Everyone left the room and she finally went over to Frank and ran her hand across his forehead and leaned down to kiss him there. He opened his eyes and smiled. He was so groggy he couldn't talk except to tell her he loved her, and then he fell back asleep. It was good that he rested.

The chaplain came in and visited with her for a minute. Having already heard the story about what happened to them, he was astounded that they survived. Shelly laughed and told him that she had already thanked "The Man Upstairs" and he laughed out loud. He went to the phone in the room and punched in a code and then let Shelly dial Frank's parent's number. She told them he was out of surgery and what the doctor had said. She asked them to call her parents and explain it to them. She would call them again when they got back to the cabin and got the other cell.

She had only been off the phone a couple of minutes when the chaplain returned and asked if he could get her anything. She hadn't even realized it until then, but she was starving and exhausted. She told him that she and Frank had eaten spaghetti around 7PM the evening before and then everything happened and she had been up all night. He told her he would show her where the cafeteria was and she could eat breakfast. He even gave her a meal voucher so that it would be free. She wasn't sure if he did it because they had had such a horrible night or if it was just hospital policy. Either way, it was very nice and she appreciated it. When he got her to the cafeteria, he told her that he would make sure the nurses would give her a fold out chair and some pillows and blankets so she could sleep when she got back to Frank's room. She gave him a hug and thanked him and went to go eat.

For a small rural hospital, they had a very good breakfast of scrambled eggs, bacon, biscuits, and white gravy. They also had pancakes and syrup in containers as well as some bowls of fruit and little boxes of cereal. There were juices and coffees and bottles of milk and soft drinks. Shelly loaded up her plate and ate like she hadn't eaten in a week. It was nourishing and comforting. She missed Frank, so she hurried to finish her coffee and got up to walk back to his room.

On the way back she yawned. She could see the sun had just risen over the mountains and the sky was a hot pink and blue. It would be a pretty day. She hated that they both had to spend it in the hospital. She yawned again.

Finally she made it to his room. He was still asleep. She saw that the chaplain had gotten her a chair and had already folded it out for her and left the sheets, blankets and pillows stacked on the nightstand for her to fix the way she wanted to. She kissed Frank on the cheek and made her bed and crawled in it and fell fast asleep. She didn't wake up even through the hospital announcements or when the nurses came in to change Frank's I.V.

It was later on in the evening when she did wake up and it was Frank that woke her.

"Hey....he said. Shelly moved her arm. Hey, Wonder Woman." Frank said.

She suddenly opened her eyes, glanced around the room, and then jumped up realizing where they were.

"Frank! I'm so glad to hear your voice. I'm so glad you're awake!" She said holding his hand.

"You saved my life. He said smiling. I had no idea you were that strong...or that mean!"

"I couldn't let him kill you...or us. I just couldn't let it happen. I had to fight. She stated matter of factly. You are my whole world."

"And you are mine. He smiled at her warmly now with tears in both of their eyes, but added, I'm so glad your fitness classes and your healthy living came in so handy!"

Shelly laughed and wiped the tears off of her face and Frank's as well. Everything was going to be okay.

They had a long night of watching TV and just talking. When it came time for the ten o'clock news, they were surprised to see that the main story was of them and what had happened. There was a news reporter standing in front of the "Hills and Hollers" office sign talking about the couple that was staying here on vacation from New York. She went on to say how Frank and Shelly had found a severed hand and had turned it in to the Mountain View Police Department, but then a few nights later, (the camera had changed scenes to right in front of their cabin which was covered in yellow crime scene tape), the serial killer that everyone had been terrified of, had tried to kill them. They then interviewed Officer Smith who had come in after Shelly had stabbed the killer with the fireplace poker. He described what he saw and why he had fired the fatal shots that finally put the man down.

"I had never seen anything like it. The officer said as he described Frank lying in a pool of blood with Shelly sitting on the floor next to him gripping the can of pepper spray, and the killer with an iron fireplace poker stuck all the way through his body, still coming after them. It was like a scene from a horror movie where you can't kill the boogeyman."

The reporter then explained that Frank had been hospitalized and was expected to make a full recovery. She closed the report saying they would be speaking with Frank and Shelly about the incident as soon as they had recovered enough and were able and willing to speak to them. She signed off with, "you'll hear it first here on this station", then they went to a commercial.

It was odd to Frank and Shelly, seeing it from that point of view, like everyone else was seeing it. It was almost like it had happened to someone else, but they knew every little detail that the reporter had left out. It sent shivers down their spines to think about it.

A nurse brought Frank some pain medication and a sedative so he could get some sleep. Shelly would have to fall asleep the natural way, but she felt like it wouldn't be a problem. She was still tired and sitting in a hospital made anyone tired in a different way. She kissed Frank goodnight and got into her pull out bed. She was asleep almost as quick as Frank.

****

Morning came with a bustle of activity from the nurses. They were checking Frank's temperature, drawing labs, and setting him up for some occupational therapy at a facility in New York that he could go to when they got home.

Until then, he was only to wiggle and flex his fingers and extend the arm a few times a day. If his lab work checked out alright, they would release him late that evening.

About three o'clock the physician that performed the surgery on Frank came and asked how he was feeling and seemed pleased to hear that Frank felt pretty good, considering. He explained that all of his labs came back within the normal ranges and didn't show any signs of anemia or infection. He felt that is was fairly safe to let him out of the hospital that day but gave them a precautionary list of things to look for such as fever or redness from the surgery site. He wanted to make sure that they were staying in town for a few more days so that they could be close to the hospital in case anything went wrong. Frank and Shelly assured him that they would be there for at least the whole week, and would return if anything seemed to go wrong. With that, he signed the discharge papers and the nurse came in and gave them more instructions and a prescription of antibiotics to go.

Since there was no taxi service, and they didn't have Cecil's truck, they wondered how they were going to get back to the cabins. They couldn't call the police department for that. It was late in the day on Monday evening. How were they going to get a ride?

"Gentry!" They both looked at each other and exclaimed.

Frank still had the business card with Gentry's cell phone number he had given to them when they were at the store. They went back inside the hospital and used a waiting room phone to make the local call. When Gentry picked up they explained their dilemma. Gentry had heard about what happened and had seen it on the news and also told them it was all over the internet and social media. He said he would be glad to take them back as soon as he closed the store, which would only be about thirty more minutes. They thanked him and said they would be waiting outside in front of the main entrance to the hospital.

It felt good to be out of the hospital and in the sun again. They were happy to be out in the fresh air. Gentry came to pick them up and they talked all the way back to the "Hills and Hollers". Gentry was blown away at their tale of what happened. They thanked him for the ride and got out of his truck in the yard of their cabin place. Their happiness was somewhat short lived when they walked through the door to the mess inside. There was still blood everywhere along with all of the opened packages of materials that the paramedics used while working on Frank. Even the furniture was in disorder and some things were broken that they had landed on when they fought. They just stood there staring. Remembering.

"Well, we need to call Cecil." Shelly stated, marching upstairs to get her cell phone that she had missed for almost two days. She came back downstairs with it and grabbed the truck keys that were on the kitchen counter by the sink where the killer, Michael Delacroix, had left them while trying to wash the pepper spray out of his eyes. She shook the thought out of her head that he was the last one to have touched them, and she and Frank walked out to the truck to make the trip up the mountain to get cell phone service. She let Frank in on the passenger side because he wouldn't be able to drive. As she was walking around the tailgate of the truck, she noticed a plastic bag in the truck bed and wondered if they had left something in it they had forgotten about. She picked up the bag and untied the knot at the top and looked in it. It had a half-eaten jar of peanut butter, a nail, a piece of wire, and a file. The serial killer's tools. He had planned on stealing their truck and making a getaway. She got in the truck and handed the bag to Frank so he could see.

    They talked about their find as they drove out to get a signal. When they finally got to a good place to call, Shelly parked the truck and turned off the ignition. She dialed Cecil's number and waited. When he answered she told him hello and asked how their vacation was and listened politely, waiting for him to ask about theirs.

    He finally did and she gave a little laugh and told him what had happened. Cecil was as shocked sounding as a country man on a cell phone could sound, and told her that they would be packing up then next day and start heading home. It would be about three days before they could finally get there because they had driven farther on down the coast to sightsee, but they would be ready to leave by morning. He expressed how happy he was that they were ok and how sorry he was that it had happened and wanted to know if there was anything they needed or he could do. Shelly told him about what a mess their cabin was and begged him to let them stay in another one because of that and the fact that just being there and remembering what happened was just too much. Cecil was more than happy to let them move to another cabin of their choice. Shelly thanked him for it and they talked a little more about how Frank was and how nice everyone had been and how Gentry had taken them back to their cabin. Cecil was glad that he had been there to help them. Finally, Shelly said goodbye to Cecil and then made a quick call to their families again telling them that Frank had been discharged from the hospital and was doing okay and that they were going to be busy, or at least she was, moving their stuff into another cabin. After that she hung up the phone and headed back down the mountain to do some work before dark.

It was all she could do to get Frank to sit still while she packed up their stuff and hauled it back out to the truck. It took a whole hour to do it and make sure they didn't leave anything behind. It felt good to walk out of there and not look at all of the evidence of what happened.

They decided to pick the Barn cabin. It was just as nice and seemed as cozy as the log cabin did when they first got there. Shelly carried their luggage in one by one and set it down on the floor of the first bedroom they came to on the downstairs. Frank had walked in and watched as she set it down and announced that she was tired. It had been morning when they had eaten a muffin at the hospital.

They had no food here except a few things they had left over in the fridge from the last cabin, and that was only soft drinks and the fixings for more sandwiches, which Shelly didn't want another one of for a while since she had eaten two at the hospital during Frank's stay. Shelly was too tired to get anything to cook, so pizza was on the list for tonight.

She let Frank stay there at the cabin while she went to pick up the pizza. He was still weak and being up the whole day had left him feeling weak. When she returned, they stuffed themselves with a deep dish pan pizza with all of the toppings and refills of Coke. It just hit the spot. They were full and ready for bed as soon as they got finished eating.

The rest of the week was just spent being quiet. Frank needed to heal. The local news station had come and done their interview with them, and they watched themselves on TV later that night and used their cell phones to video it so they could show their friends and family. They would really get a kick out of that. They bought several movies, bought some games to play, and another book to read. They enjoyed walks around the property, noticing the spring flowers that Cecil and his family had planted in various flower beds in their yard. They had fun cooking some more meals together in the kitchen that was decorated with chickens and painted in warm beige, orange, and a rustic red that made you feel cozy just looking at it.

Cecil and his family arrived on Thursday and had a long visit with Frank and Shelly and went with them over to the Log cabin to see what happened. Cecil had already contacted a professional company that cleaned up crime scenes and asked them what he needed to clean up the place, since there was no company anywhere close to Mountain View that specialized in that. He needed to go get some biohazard grade trash bags and the proper gloves and clothing to wear while cleaning it, as well as the right chemicals to clean up all the blood with. He had already been in contact with the hospital about disposing of it there along with their biohazard trash. He was still in a state of disbelief about what happened, and applauded Frank and Shelly for how well they had fought and thanked them for taking care of the place like they had, and even apologized saying if he had known that was going to happen, he would've never agreed to them staying. They had almost gotten killed. He was almost in tears at what they went through.

Earlier on, Frank had called his office and told them that he would have to take a little more time off from work. He had plenty of sick leave and they encouraged him to use it and agreed that he needed to relax. He and Shelly had originally planned to fly back home on Sunday at the end of that week, but decided to stay until Tuesday. When they got back to New York, Frank would take some additional days off and get started in therapy.

They had been hanging around watching Cecil make repairs to the cabins that were damaged and watched some of the cleanup of the Log cabin. Cecil had a lot to do to get ready for new renters. They hoped that what had happened there wouldn't deter people from wanting to rent a cabin at the Hills and Hollers. One day, Cecil's wife came to their cabin with a basket of fruit and a bouquet of fresh flowers that had come for Frank. It was from the couple they had met at the Court Square on Friday night that had invited them to their church. They had heard about what happened and saw their interview on the news and wanted to show their support. It was a very sweet gesture and Frank and Shelly were overwhelmed.

Sunday

Chapter 15

It was around noon on Saturday when they were talking about what they were going to do the next couple of days before they flew back home to New York when they decided that they would go to visit the church they were invited to for Sunday morning service. Shelly washed their nice clothes and ironed them so they would look presentable, and when they both put them on the next morning they each bragged on the other's appearance. They also noticed that they would have to go on a diet very soon.

On Sunday morning they drove out to the church and parked at the far end of the parking lot under a tree. They were there a few minutes before 11am and slipped in quietly and sat on the back pew. The service was started with the singers that they had heard at the Court Square and they sang just as beautiful here if not better. Frank and Shelly sat holding hands, enjoying the peacefulness. When the pastor got up to give the sermon he spoke about God being their protector in their times of trouble and how you were to call on Him when you needed help. Shelly remembered her prayer for Frank while he was in surgery and that even though she was alone, she felt comforted. She also wondered as she sat there listening, that since they had already been thinking about going to this church service, even though their lives hadn't been disrupted yet by the serial killer, that maybe God had, in essence, laid His protective hand over them that night and kept the serial killer from doing any more harm than he did. Maybe God was protecting them for no other reason, except that they acknowledged that He existed and knew they wanted to have a relationship with Him.

It was a nice service and when it was over they shook hands with the other members as they were walking out the door. They saw the couple that had invited them and thanked them for the fruit basket and flowers. They talked as they walked out to their vehicles and got to know more about each other. Like everyone else they had met and gotten to know, they exchanged e-mails and decided to keep in touch.

After lunch they went for a drive around Mountain View. They talked about all the things they had done here on their vacation and about how much fun they'd had and how pretty it was here. They regretted they hadn't gotten to go fishing. Crazy as it seemed, and even with what happened, they were glad they had gotten to enjoy a vacation away from the big city. People were so nice here and they had made so many friends. They were anxious to get back home to see their families, but they hated to leave what they had found.

Before they went back to the Barn cabin, Frank grabbed a local newspaper just to see what it had in it. There might be something they missed out on seeing or doing that they could do tomorrow.

When they got back to the Hills and Hollers, they saw a patrol car parked at the office and wondered what was going on. They pulled in and stopped next to it and got out. The

Sergeant that had been on duty the night they found the body came out of the office door and walked towards them.

"I was just looking for you." He said smiling.

"I'm not sure if that's good or bad!" Frank kidded.

"It's nothing bad. Just wanted to pass along some news to you. Normally we don't do this, but since you survived a situation that was so gruesome and I know from hearing your statements and hearing the officer that shot Mr. Delacroix, that it did traumatize you in some way, he said looking at Shelly, that I thought you needed to hear this. You needed to know that what happened wasn't your fault, or anyone's for that matter."

It had bothered Shelly that she had killed a man, even if she did it to save her own and Frank's life. Michael Delacroix's words still rang in her ears and haunted her; "I'm sorry for what I've done. Please bury me by my mother".

"The Carroll Parish Sheriff's Department has been back out to where Mr. Delacroix lived, while the man hunt was still going on, to see if they could find out more about him. Where he might go when he was running. See if they could find out where he might be running to. Anyway, they found a notebook that he had been writing in, a diary of sorts. Every page was dated. He had started writing in it over five years ago. The things that he was writing about then seemed pretty normal. He had written that he had finally paid off the place that he lived in and was making good money at an automotive station where he worked on cars. He mentions that he wished his daddy could see what he'd made of himself and that if he knew how successful he had become then maybe he wouldn't have ran off and left them back when he was just a kid, but that it was alright because he had his mother and she was proud of him. A little ways on over, he talks about meeting a lady and going out on a date with her and that he really liked her. They kept going out and he talked about maybe asking her to marry him eventually but just couldn't do it yet. He was enjoying what they had at the moment. Then it starts to get bad. He had started having headaches and started hearing voices. At first he stated that they were just normal voices like people you hear talking in the background and that he would turn and look and nobody would be there. Or he would think it was one of the guys he worked with telling him something and would ask them what they said, and nobody had said anything to him. It made him feel embarrassed, so he stopped talking all together except for work related questions that he *had* to ask. He went to a doctor and they diagnosed him with either Schizophreniform Disorder, hope I said that right, or as being bipolar. We looked it up on the computer. Schizopreniform disorder is a disorder that's a whole lot like schizophrenia, but is a little different. You are still able to function, which is why he still had his job, up until he just started killing people that one day, and if the symptoms resolve, then the disorder can be downgraded, but if they persist, then the person is upgraded to real schizophrenia.

Bipolar, it says, has a lot of different criteria and subtypes and that's one of the reasons that they weren't sure of the diagnosis because after they saw him just a few times, he stopped going and stopped taking the medications they had prescribed to him because his mother had been diagnosed with cancer and he had to spend all of the time he had and money he made helping her. He wrote in his diary how scared he was of her dying and that his girlfriend had left him because she was afraid of him and his mood swings, and that he was talking to voices that only he heard. After his mother died, he really lost it. His writing became very dark. He talked about how bad he felt as a person. That nothing mattered anymore. He tried to make it better and thought that going to church might help, and in his opinion it did. He wrote that God had given him a new mission in life…to kill people that did not deserve to live because they didn't believe in God. He got it twisted in his head that God told him to go out and kill these people. I guess, somewhere in whatever illness he had, whether it was Schizophreniform or Bipolar Disorder, he flip-flopped between being nice and caring, to being a ruthless killer because he thought he was told to kill. He was just on a bad path that more than likely would've eventually led to this in one way or the other because he couldn't stop doing what he was doing. I'm not sure if he'd have been this way if he had continued taking his medication or not, but you had no choice but to do what you did. He would have killed you."

    Shelly was glad to hear the explanation, but was still sad. The best case scenario would've been for him to have gotten captured by the police alive and taken to jail and then possibly committed to a mental institution and given medications. It would've given him a chance to possibly be normal again, even if he did have to spend the rest of his life in prison or an institution for the murders, but it didn't happen that way. She knew he was a killer, but some part of her down deep just couldn't help feeling bad for him.

    "They did bury his body by his mother, so he got his final wish. The Sergeant told them. And the hitchhiker that he killed was shipped home to his relatives. I guess that's all there is to the whole thing now."

They thanked him again for letting them know everything. He told them that he hoped that Frank would get better soon and that they enjoyed the rest of their vacation here and not to let that incident change their perspective on their usually quiet little town. He invited them to come back again for another vacation. They assured him that they had really loved the town and had enjoyed Mountain View so much and made so many friends and met so many nice people that they dreaded to go home. He shook hands with them as he turned to get in his patrol car and said goodbye.

That night as they sat around going back over their photos that they had taken and counting up all of the e-mail addresses they had collected and name additions to social media, they started talking about all the people they had met. They had seen each person in town several times over and had gotten to know them better. They were all unique in their own way. Then they talked about places in town they had been to or seen that they liked or that were special to them in some way or another. Some places were special because they had eaten there or shopped there, but some were special because of the way the land looked or the trees or flowers on the property. In May, several things were blooming and the leaves on the trees were a bright green. Lush grass covered the ground and was scattered with crimson clover.

There were several old home places where someone used to live years ago that still had old rock houses and in the yards, there were bright purple clumps of phlox surrounding tree trunks that someone had planted years ago, and wild rosebushes climbing the corners of the houses or an old barbed wire fence whose wooden posts were rotting from decades of weather. Frank and Shelly had gotten out at a few of them just to take photos. They were pretty in a haunting sort of way. Long after the person was gone, the place and its flowers still remained.

Frank reached over on the end of the couch and got the newspaper he'd gotten earlier that day and was skimming through it. They had pretty much covered all there was to do in Mountain View and then some. He came to the classified section and was looking at the real estate adds.

"Hmm." He grunted. Shelly glanced over at him and then back to what she was doing.

"Hmmmm!" He made the same noise again, only this time louder and more enthusiastic. She finally asked him what he had found.

"There are some places for sale here in town and I hadn't even wondered what property or houses might cost here, but surprisingly, they aren't that expensive. Some are under a hundred thousand and some just a little over that. Of course there are some that are full farms that are hundreds of thousands, but the others are reasonable."

Shelly looked over sideways and read a few of them. "Do you want to look at some of them just for the fun of it?" She asked.

"Sure! How about tomorrow?"

"Ok with me." She smiled.

Early the next morning they got up and ate a light breakfast of bagels with coffee. It was nice not to have to go check all of the cabins now that Cecil was back. They grabbed the newspaper and got in the truck and went in search of a real estate office. They knew without it they would never be able to find the properties.

There was an office on Main Street and the agent, a man in his late fifties asked them what kind of properties they would like to see. They gave him a price range of sixty thousand to one hundred thousand to start with. He showed them several houses off of the main road. Some of them down dirt roads. Some with no air conditioning. Some with an old wood stove that had a ring of black soot all around the stove pipe that looked like the ceiling could go up in flames the next time they built a fire. He took them to some quaint little cottage style houses closer to town that they liked more. On the way to another property, Frank and Shelly both pointed out the window to one of the old homesteads they had seen and had admired from the road. It was a property off by itself with a barbed wire fence surrounding it and a large field behind it with trees at the very back of the property. There was an old stone house still there, but the roof had caved in and all of the windows had long been broken out.

"How about that one?" Frank almost shouted.

"That?" The realtor asked in shock.

"Yep, that." Frank answered with a smile.

"Well, I'm not even sure that property is for sale. Let me look. He said as he took out his computer and pulled up the listings. Well, I don't see it in here. I'm sorry."

"Do you know who owns the property?" Frank asked.

"I'm not sure, but I'll try and find out for you. Are you sure you like it? That would be a lot of work and a lot of money to fix up. There's almost nothing there but just the frame of rock."

Frank looked at Shelly and then back at the realtor. "Yes, sir. We just like the way it looks and it could be beautiful."

"Well, ok. Let's stop at a couple of places up the road and see if those folks know who might own it. That will give you a start."

First they stopped at the next house down the road and it was a younger couple that didn't know who owned the property. They said that the old man across the road might know who had owned it because he had lived here all of his life. They got back in the car and drove over to that house and the realtor got out and knocked on the door. Finally an elderly white haired gentleman came to the door and they talked for about ten minutes before the realtor came and got back in his vehicle. He put the key in the ignition and started the car and began backing out of the driveway before he spoke.

"He said that he had indeed lived here all of his life and that the old couple that had lived in that house passed away over ten years ago. He thought that they had left the place to his son. Well, his son has been in the nursing home for the last two years, as he was old himself and he has an only child, a daughter that lives here in town." He explained.

"Do you know where she lives?" Shelly asked

"Sure do, and we're headed there now. In fact, I know her well. She bought her own house from us years ago. She's a very nice lady."

They drove back through town and down the road past Hipp Modern Builders. Another mile down the road they turned off onto a gravel driveway and up to a nice brick house.

This time he asked Frank and Shelly to go up to the door with him so they could ask her about the place. The realtor knocked on the door and in less than a few seconds she opened it.

"Hello Mary. How are you doing?" He asked shaking her hand as she smiled, obviously recognizing him.

"I'm doing fine Bill, what brings you out here?" She asked glancing at Frank and Shelly.

"Well, this young couple have been here on vacation for the last two weeks, in fact you might have seen them on the news..." he started, but didn't get to finish because Mary had recognized them immediately after he said that.

"Anyway, he finally got back to the point, they have enjoyed our town so much that they are thinking of buying a house here." He finished.

"Well, this house isn't for sale. She answered looking a little puzzled, but still smiling.

"It's not this house that we're interested in." Shelly told her.

"But I don't own another house?" She stated looking

even more puzzled.

Frank finally spoke up. "It's the property on the other end of town with the old stone house. Do you own that ma'am?" He asked politely.

"My grandparent's old place? My daddy owned it, but he's in the nursing home and he doesn't even know what's going on anymore. He has dementia. He deeded that place over to me a couple of years before he went in there because he could see what was happening to him and he didn't want the nursing home to get it in case he did end up going. He thought that my husband and myself might want to use it someday to raise cattle on, but we just don't have the time and don't really need it for that. It's just been sitting there like it is because there wasn't anything we could really do with it and I thought my kids might want it, but they have other dreams besides living in Mountain View." She chuckled.

"Well, is it for sale ma'am?" Frank asked.

"You know, I haven't thought about it in some time. I hated to get rid of it because it was my grandparents place and I have so many good memories there and I knew that someone would tear the house down and change the place up so that I just never did sell it, but it's just sitting there not doing anyone any good." She said.

"We wouldn't tear down the house ma'am. Frank told her as she looked at him surprised.

"We really love it." Shelly added.

"We would really like to fix it up and add on to it. We don't want to change it very much at all. A new roof and maybe a couple of rooms added on to the back of the house. We haven't even been inside it yet, but I think we could make it look really nice. Keep the rock walls and put a coat of clear sealer on it and it would be beautiful. Frank explained. We would even hope you would come out and tell us about the house. What each room was. What it meant to you and the things you remember. And even get your opinion on what things we were doing to it. You would be welcome any time."

Tears started to run down Mary's cheeks at what Frank said and she smiled and began wiping them away quickly and then laughed.

"We love it here in Mountain View. Shelly said to her. And we would be honored to live in such a pretty place as your grandparents did."

Mary burst into laughter and tears all at the same time and excused herself for just a moment and left the realtor and Frank and Shelly standing on the porch looking around at each other and smiling. In just a minute she came back with her husband and a handful of tissues and began to talk.

I told my husband about what you want and your idea. He doesn't mind what I do with the property and told me to make my own decision on it, and you know, Mary said, that property isn't doing anyone any good like it is. Daddy will never go back to it, and I'm just letting it run down by not being able to use it like it needs to be. You seem like a nice couple and I'm flattered that you love the place so much and honored that you would want me and my memories to help you make it beautiful. I would be happy to sell it to someone who would allow me to come and visit and I would be glad for someone to love the place like I have. I would be willing to sell it to you!"

"That's great!" Frank and Shelly exclaimed shaking her hand.

The realtor didn't really have anything to do with the sale, so Frank and Shelly thanked him for taking them around to find the owner and told him that he could take them back to the real estate office to get the truck and they would come back on their own so he could go back to work. They paid him fifty dollars just for the trouble he went through in helping them and then they got in the truck to drive back to Mary's house.

She invited them in and they talked for hours about who they all were and where Frank and Shelly were from and got to know all about each other. Finally, Mary went and got the deed to the property and told them that they had had it appraised at one time and it was worth $150,000 for just the land, which happened to be eighty acres of prime pasture. The house was worth nothing in value, but a lot in memories. Mary wondered if they were still interested in it for that amount.

Frank and Shelly asked her to excuse them for a few minutes and they went outside to Cecil's truck to talk it over. They had saved way more than that for their own "perfect" house that they would live in in New York, so they would still have some money left over for that and they could save a little extra and take a little more time if they wanted to or pay it off when they wanted to as well. Mountain View already seemed like home in a way and they knew they would be mad at themselves if they didn't buy it. It would only be a home for vacations when they wanted to get away and if they ever did want to quit the businesses they were in, they could always move there and work somewhere else. For right now, they just wanted the place.

Lift Off

Chapter 16

They went back in and sat back down at the kitchen table with Mary and her husband. They looked at each other, and then looked back at Mary and said, "We want it!"

Instead of shaking hands she got up and gave both of them a hug. They told her they would mail her a check as soon as they got back home to New York and then she could mail them the title. They exchanged addresses and all of the necessary information and then Frank and Shelly got up to leave. It had been a pleasure meeting Mary and her husband and the feeling with them was mutual. They had made more new friends.

They got back in the truck and was driving back to their cabin when they saw the sign for Hipp Modern Builders up ahead. Frank whipped in to the parking lot.

"We need to pay Gentry one more visit." he said smiling.

They got out and went in. Gentry was behind the counter talking to a customer and saw them walk in.

"Be with ya'll in a minute." He said as he finished writing up the order that the customer had given him. "Ya'll out looking for another serial killer today?" He teased.

"No thanks!" Shelly said with her eyes bugged out, then laughed.

"Actually, we wanted to stop by and say goodbye and

wanted to get your e-mail address or find out which social media to contact you on. We would love to keep in touch." Frank said.

"Well come on in to my office and I'll write down my e-mail and yes, I'm on everything. Gentry said with an air of silly dignity. So ya'll are going back to New York? He asked.

"Yes, for now. Frank explained, but we'll be back. As a matter of fact, we also need you for business purposes…we bought a house while we are here!"

He explained where it was and told Gentry what kind of shape it was in and what plans they had for it and they would be needing his expertise on a lot of stuff since they had no experience in building at all, but just knew what they wanted it to look like when it was finished. They also told him that he would be getting all of their business when it came to buying materials for fixing it up. Gentry was happy to hear that and told them he would help them all he could and could give them the names and numbers of some local carpenters and electricians as well.

When they got ready to leave Frank told Gentry it was great meeting him and that he appreciated all that he had done to help them and for the ride back to the cabins from the hospital. Gentry said he had been glad to do it and asked them when they would be coming back to Mountain View to start on their house. They explained what kind of work they did and that Frank's arm needed a little time to get better first, so he could help work on the house. They figured about five months would be a good time to take another break and fly down. They would keep in touch and let him know. Gentry told them that the next time they were here, he would invite them up to his own house in Prim with his wife and kids and grill out. Frank and Shelly were excited to do that. They told him about their trip through Prim and about seeing the round rocks. They finally said goodbye to Gentry and went back to town and down the mountain to their cabin. They stopped by the office first and talked to Cecil for a few minutes to see what progress he had made on patching up the Victorian Cabin and on Cleaning the Log Cabin. He said that the Victorian Cabin was finished and ready to rent out, but the Log Cabin was still a work in progress.

"Funny thing though, Cecil started, "We've been getting calls all week from people that want to book a cabin rental. They've all heard about what happened with the serial killer and ya'll. As crazy as it sounds, they all want to rent *that* cabin! Guess it's kinda like stayin in a celebrity suit in a fancy hotel. Instead of people stayin away from it, they want to be in it! Think we'll rename it "Serial Killer Cabin" until all the fuss about it is over!"

Frank and Shelly were amazed but happy at the news that Cecil wouldn't have a decrease in customers from the incident. He might even get rich if he promoted it the right way. They told him about what they had been doing that day and about the property they bought. He was excited to hear it and was glad they had liked being in Mountain View that much. He said he would be glad to see them again and if they needed somewhere to stay while they worked on the house, they were welcome to stay in one of the cabins rent free while they did.

They thanked him sincerely and then told him that they

were going back to their cabin to pack. They had called the airlines and set up a time to fly home the next day and asked Cecil if he could take them to the airport in the truck again. Cecil told them he would be glad to.

They said goodnight to him and went back to begin their task. It took a while since they had accumulated more stuff during their stay. By ten o'clock they were ready to go to bed.

Their jet would be at the airport at 11AM. Frank and Shelly had been up and ready to go by 9AM. They had eaten the last of the breakfast groceries they had bought for the week and had cleaned up the cabin best they could. They had all of their luggage and bags piled on the front porch and ready to go when Cecil came to get them. His wife brought him in their other vehicle and dropped him off so he could use the truck to come back in. She said her goodbye's to them and gave them a hug, then jumped back in the Land Rover to get back to the office.

"Looks like ya'll are all ready to go." Cecil said.

"Yep, I think we got it all." Frank laughed as Cecil helped him and Shelly put everything in the bed of the truck. Frank could only use his good arm to carry and lift.

"How's the arm?" Cecil asked.

"It's still sore and stiff and feels numb right here and here. Frank pointed to his arm and fingers. It feels a lot better than it did though and I feel stronger."

"Glad to hear it. Cecil said. You'll be alright in no time. Just don't hurt it doing too much." he cautioned.

They finally got everything loaded and all climbed in the truck. They had a nice ride to the airport and Cecil made sure they still had his number and told them to give him a call when they were ready to come back. He'd make sure the truck had gas in it so they could use it again.

"Tell that niece of mine that she could visit once in a while too!" He joked, then gave Shelly a hug and gave Frank a vigorous handshake telling them to keep in touch and said goodbye.

Their jet was there in a few minutes and again they had to load their luggage onto the small plane. They had the same pilot as before and he joked with them about having so much stuff the jet would be too heavy to lift off.

When they were finally seated and seat belted in, the jet roared down the runway and blasted off into the sky. Frank and Shelly looked down below them as the tiny town got even smaller. Mountain View would forever be in their memories and in their hearts. They had experienced life there in a different way than they ever knew before, in so many different ways, and had almost experienced death. It brought them closer together and made them appreciate what they had in life and in each other. They couldn't wait to see their family and friends and knew that they would be coming back to Mountain View very soon.

The End

Made in the USA
Lexington, KY
28 November 2015